The Monroe Sisters

LET ME GO

ALIYAH BURKE

Let Me Go
ISBN # 978-1-78686-386-7
©Copyright Aliyah Burke 2019
Cover Art by Erin Dameron-Hill ©Copyright January 2019
Interior text design by Claire Siemaszkiewicz
Totally Bound Publishing

LET ME GO

Dedication

To my very own amazing DH,
the one I know wouldn't let me go.

Chapter One

Tara rubbed the back of her neck and sighed. *Christ, I could be here for another six hours and not feel like I've made any progress.*

She wanted to head home and crawl into bed, but she had work to finish and now a visitor. Someone who she would be fine shooting for the pain he had inflicted on her older sister.

The knock came and she set down the gold pen. "Come on in."

"Don't stay too long now, Ms. Monroe," Marcus the security guard said.

She lifted her head and gave him a smile. "You know me, Marcus. Here until the job is done."

As she sliced her gaze to the left of the kind man, ice formed in her veins, and while the smile on her face never slipped an inch, she had no doubt the warmth in her eyes had vanished.

Grant Harrison.

She and Marcus made some small talk before he left her alone in the room with Grant. Silence stretched between them and she would have been content to let it go on. However she truly longed for a hot bath, wine and bed.

"What are you doing here, Mr. Harrison?"

"Looking for your sister. She wasn't at the hospital nor her place."

And now that you want her, it's pissing you off that you can't find her.

Tara reclined in her chair, steepled her fingers and exhaled sharply with irritation. "Let me get this straight, make sure I have all the facts. You were supposed to come be with her over Christmas, yet instead of being a man about it, you ran out of the country and didn't call her until after you'd landed in Uruguay. During which point there wasn't really anything further for you to say, aside from how sorry you were." She leaned forward, hands clasped on her smooth desktop, fingers laced. "What the hell makes you think I would help you find her and not have you thrown in jail?"

Can I just punch him in the face?

He drew back a slight bit, eyebrows converging and a slight concern in his expression. "Jail? For what?"

"Whatever charge I want to trump up on you." She spread her hands over the desk. "You hurt my sister. Made her cry. I don't like you."

"I know what I did was wrong. May I sit?" He waited a few seconds before taking a chair, even though she never gave her agreement. "I was a pussy and I hid from my feelings. I want to explain this to her and move on."

"You expected her to what? Just wait for you to come to your senses? In case you haven't noticed, Doctor, my sister is a damn fine catch. It's not like there aren't other men who would be happy to have her in their life. Besides, she's moved on from you."

She had to give him credit—he didn't flinch, not once, at her words. Perhaps she'd underestimated him.

Tara didn't let up. "In fact, for all I know, she's in bed with someone right now, enjoying his—"

"I get it." The words rolled from his mouth on a growl.

She smirked, enjoying his immense discomfort. "Do you? Really? She's not going to take you back."

"Yes." The single word was uttered with a sharp undertone and his expression reminded her of someone who'd swallowed something foul. "I get your point. She could be with someone else."

She reached for her gold pen and twirled it in her fingers before pointing it in his direction. "And happy. She could be happy. Don't forget that. That is extremely important for you to remember. Her *happiness*."

"I get it." His tone got sharper and he frowned again. "Why won't she take me back?"

She quirked an eyebrow, unfazed by his attitude and surliness. "Wanted to make sure you understood. I *don't* like you, Grant. You hurt *my* sister. Had her believing in you and how you were going to treat her right. She had fallen in love with you and you, what did you do? You broke her heart. Now that would be enough of a reason, but there's more."

His head snapped up, hope alive in his gaze. "She loves me?"

She waved a hand. "I said she'd *fallen* in love with you, not that she still was *in* love with you. Not that it matters, she won't allow you back in."

"Where is she, Tara?"

"I'm sure you think that doctor tone will get you what you want and for some it may. Trouble is, I have a sister who's a doctor, and I'm used to the tone. Plus, I have one who teaches for a living and she is a master at that no-nonsense tone, so stuff it away, you don't intimidate me."

His hands clenched into fists and he took several deep breaths. "I have no desire to intimidate you. I want to know where Eva is, so I can talk to her."

This is actually fun. Tara leaned back and watched him. "I want you to understand the only reason I'm telling you anything about her is because I saw how hurt she was when you blew her off."

"I didn't blow her off."

Tara snapped upright, hands landing on the desk with a loud slap. "Bullshit. You could have told her you were leaving the country well before you did, not calling once you were there. That's blowing her off and not truly pertinent to this discussion. I'm talking to you, and if you're smart, you will be listening."

Grant ground his jaw but remained silent. He held up his hands then gestured for her to continue.

"She's down in Orlando."

"For?"

"Does it matter?" Condemnation lined her tone.

"No, it doesn't."

Tara picked up a sheet of paper and wrote something down then slid it over the desk to him. "I hear you hurt her again and I swear I will make you pay."

"An assistant district attorney making idle threats?"

Her eyebrow jacked up and she began to rise and nail him to the seat with nothing more than a glare. "Trust me, this is no idle threat. Yes, I'm an ADA but first and foremost, I'm a sister and I *hate* the fact you've hurt *my* sister."

"Everything okay here, Ms. Monroe?"

Grant turned even though she didn't move from her position.

"We're fine, Marcus," she replied. "He was just leaving."

Snapping up the paper, he didn't even bother looking at it, just got to his feet and shoved it into his pocket. "Thank you."

"Thank me by doing the right thing. Leave her alone after you say whatever you have to get off your chest. Let her get on with her life." She dropped her gaze to the papers in front of her, making it very clear that he was no longer wanted in the office.

The door closed behind them and she sighed with frustration. Reaching for the phone, she debated calling Eva to give her a heads-up on what she'd just done.

If I do that, she'll find a way to hide from him and she needs to resolve her issues before she can allow herself to move on with her life. Tara snorted.

"Because I'm a fine one to tell anyone about facing your past to allow yourself to move on with the future." She scrubbed a hand down her face. "I'm such a fraud."

Phone in hand, she punched a familiar number.

"What's wrong?" Shai asked, answering on the first ring.

"Harrison was just here in my office."

"Fuck," she snapped. "What happened? Did you throw him in jail?"

She smiled and chuckled. "I thought about it, but no, I didn't. I gave him Eva's information on where she is in Orlando."

Shai didn't say a word and Tara rolled her lower lip in her teeth as she waited.

"Probably for the best." Shai's comment came after a moment's pause. "She still loves him."

Tara couldn't explain the relief that filled her at her sister's support. "Thank God you feel that way too. I mean, I made him sweat a bit, but I did give it to him and I'm not calling her."

"Good. She'd just find a way to disappear."

"Exactly what I was thinking." She rubbed her neck. "Thank you, Shai. I mean, I love her and she's our sister, but she has to face him, face her past. She can't keep running from him."

"I'm glad you think you shouldn't be running from your past."

All the air sucked from her body in the space of time it took that sentence to register in her head.

"Shit," she whispered.

"Tara? You okay?" Shai's question rang in her ear.

She looked at the man who'd just entered her office as if he had the right to be there. A dark gray suit that had been tailored just for him. His close-cropped beard didn't even have a hair out of place. It never did. This man didn't know how to be messy or anything less than one hundred percent together.

His lapis-blue eyes locked on her and her hand trembled, actually trembled, as she tried not to drop the phone.

"Tara Lynne, talk to me or I'm calling the cops."

"Hang up the phone, Tara." He tugged once on the cuff of his suit coat.

"I'm fine, Shai. I have to go, there's someone in my office."

"Who? Who's there?"

"My husband."

She put the phone back on the cradle. Licking her lips, she allowed her gaze to run over him once more. *Damn, he's just as fine as the day I up and left him.*

"What the hell are you doing back here in my life, Coleman?"

Baron Andrew Coleman stared at his little spitfire of a wife. Five years and not a goddamn word from her. She had never once reached out to him for money, for help, or even to ask for a divorce. Not that it would have mattered — he wasn't going to divorce her. She was his wife and it was time for her to act like it.

"That's not exactly the proper greeting for husband and wife." He moved closer, taking in the woman before him sitting at the large desk, papers all over it. Skimming his gaze over the name plaque there — 'Tara Monroe, Assistant District Attorney'. It matched the 'ADA' on the door.

It gnawed at him she wasn't using his name, but that was a fight for him to address later. He reached out and touched her pink bangs. She didn't move, neither closer nor back to him. She just watched.

"This is new."

Her expression cooled and grew calculating. The phone beside her rang and she picked it up.

"I'm fine, Shai. I'll explain everything later tonight. Yes, I'll come over as soon as I get him out of my office. I promise."

Tara never looked away from him the entire time she spoke to Shai. One of her sisters, if he remembered correct. *Who am I kidding? I know everything about her.* And he did. When she'd left him, he had taken great pains to find out everything he could about her and her family, just in case she needed him.

Pulling out one of the chairs, he looked at it before lowering himself to the leather. She narrowed her eyes at him as she hung up the phone.

"I hardly see how my hair color is of any relevance. What are you doing here?"

"I've come to bring my wife home."

He stared at her, hoping for some kind of expression, but was disappointed that there wasn't even a flare of heat.

If anything, her gaze grew colder. "I'm not going anywhere with you. However, you are more than welcome to head out this door and never come back."

Hell, just being back in her presence fueled his blood. He'd missed her every second they'd been apart. *I was an idiot to let this go on so long.*

"Do you really think I am going to let you continue to ignore the fact we are married?"

She shrugged as if she didn't give a damn one way or the other.

"You are a Baroness and should be living with your husband."

Her left eye twitched. A sign he'd learned meant she was struggling to remain in control of her temper. On a personal level, he loved when she lost it. Tara Coleman was a wildcat and he loved being at the receiving end of her fire. Especially when it pertained to time in the bedroom. Or wherever he had the privilege of being sunk all the way within her heat.

"That title came as a repercussion of the marriage vows. It will be attached to me whether or not we are living in the same place. As I stated when we first started this asinine argument of how you want me at home all the time to be ready to fuck you whenever you decide, that's not my life. It won't be my life and you're wasting both our time if you think for one moment that I've changed my mind about that. So, I'm happy to divorce you and relieve myself of that title, or you can turn your ass around, head back to Switzerland or wherever you're living at now and leave me the fuck alone to continue what I love doing. Being with family and my job."

"There won't be any divorce and you'll come home."

There. He stated it with complete calm.

"Just because you have a title doesn't mean you get to ignore what you don't want to hear. Marriage doesn't mean I obey blindly. It's called the twenty-first century and women are allowed to say no to men, even their husbands, regardless of how some may feel."

Frustration welled up within him. This wasn't supposed to take any time. She was supposed to agree and they would be back on his plane. Andrew stroked his chin and rested one foot on his knee.

"You don't need to work, I am more than capable of taking care of you and providing anything you want. However, I grow tired of having to jack off every night because you are not there with me. You are my wife, Tara, and you should be at your husband's side."

"I happen to like working. I love my job and I'm not giving it up for you. Definitely not because you are tired of jacking off. I don't give a damn. Do it, don't do it, makes no difference to me." She slammed the file on her desk closed and pushed to her feet. "Or pay someone to do it. Again, I don't care."

He rose out of manners without thought. Andrew followed her gaze to her jacket and was there to help her put it on. He let her comment go, hearing the edge in her words when she said to allow another's touch on him. That wouldn't be happening, because he couldn't stomach the thought, and he knew damn sure that, were the situations reversed, he would kill another man for touching her.

"Thank you," she whispered as he released the woolen material to settle upon her shoulders.

His eyelids drifted closed as her soft scent wafted to his nose. Cherry blossom and a hint of white sandalwood. The only reason he knew it was because he'd had it made up for her specially when they had been on their honeymoon. When they'd gotten back, he'd given her all the information to get more if she wanted—since he smelled it now, he knew she had. And like it had then, now, it stirred his groin.

He followed her out of the door and waited as she shut it then double-checked the lock.

"We need to talk about this, Tara."

"We don't, actually. Now, if you'll excuse me, I have things to do and people to see." She skimmed him with her gaze and at last he found some heat in her expression. However quick it was, he *saw* it. "It was good to see you."

She headed off down the hall, her heels clicking with each confident stride. Andrew stood there and watched, *again*, as his wife walked away from him, determined to keep him out of her life.

Not happening again, Tara.

A man walked into view at the end of the hall and she stopped to talk to him. Jealousy churned in his gut when she tipped back her head and laughed. He lengthened his stride and made it to her in time to hear her conversation with the guard.

"This man will need to be escorted out, Marcus. I'm leaving and I'm pretty sure he's not here to see anyone else."

"Yes, Ms. Monroe. I will see you tomorrow—have a good night."

She reached out and squeezed his arm. "I will, heading off to spend some time with my sister. Give my best to your wife."

Tara didn't even allow him the satisfaction of another glance, just walked off down the hall. When he made to follow her, the guard named Marcus got in his way and gestured to the elevator.

He angled back in time to see her vanish around the corner. The guard cleared his throat and used his head to encourage Andrew to get into the waiting car.

She was in for a huge surprise if she thought this was over.

Chapter Two

Tara rode in silence to her sister's house. Her insides were a complete disaster and if she'd had any heartburn medicine, she would've ingested the entire bottle. Probably gone to look for a second after that.

How dare he? After all these years, how dare he come back and disrupt the life I've made for myself?

With a few shuddering breaths, she flexed her fingers upon the steering wheel and did her best to calm down. It would do her no good to be worked up when she faced Shai. She was in for some tough questioning.

And she deserved it. No doubt in her mind.

Pulling off the interstate that had taken her to the other side of town, she slowed on the side streets into her sister's neighborhood. Shai lived in a quiet place and was the only one of the sisters who'd made the leap to purchase a house. She and Eva had lived in apartments, but Shai wanted a place to call her own.

Turning into the drive, she then parked in front of the garage door and killed the lights. Another couple of deep breaths before she was able to turn the key, swipe her bag and climb out.

The outside light was on seconds after she shut her driver's door. Her sister appeared on the porch, long fingers curved around a cup of what she was damn near positive was coffee. The enormity of the situation weighed on her, even heavier now. Each step she took toward her sister increased the pressure tenfold upon her chest.

"Coffee's ready. And the dessert is set out, although I suspect you haven't had any real food all day so I also have a salad for you."

That was it. That was Shai's way of saying she had a little bit longer before she had to come clean on everything that she hadn't said over the phone. Tara was pretty sure this was because Eva wasn't here to join in the tag team.

Once inside Shai's three-bedroom rambler, she put her briefcase down on the chair by the door, shrugged out of her coat and turned to give her sister a hug before she hung it up.

"Thank you for letting me eat first."

Shai didn't say anything, just stared at her and arched a finely plucked eyebrow. Then she sipped some coffee and walked to the kitchen, where she sat down beside the place setting with the salad and a glass of wine.

Tara went straight for the wine, drank it all quick, and set the glass down with a sheepish grin. Light jazz played in the background. Her stomach growled and she dug into the grilled shrimp salad.

Her sister waited, by all appearances unconcerned with anything else, but allowing her the time to eat.

With this kind of patience, she would've made one hell of an attorney. She would just wait everybody else out.

There was no more wine offered through the meal. However, as she finished her last bite of salad, a fresh cup of coffee was set before her. And she knew it was fixed the way she enjoyed it. Strong and sweet.

Curving her hands around the porcelain that depicted symbols of algebraic equations she couldn't ever begin to understand, she allowed the heat to sink into her. Fixating on the cookies that had somehow appeared between her and Shai, she took a deep breath and lifted her gaze to focus on her sister's dark brown eyes.

The dark violet streak in her hair gave her an edgy look that suited her so well.

"So I'm married."

"If that was your attempt at a humorous opening it fell short."

For a second she wished Eva was there. Her oldest sister would've laughed, finding it amusing, but Shai had a very dry sense of humor and in actuality didn't laugh all that much. There were times when it was just the three of them that she would let her guard down and show off the side that the world typically did not get to see. It was kind of unique considering she had a streak of color throughout her hair while she taught at the university.

"I know. And I know I owe you, Eva—hell, Mom and Dad for sure—an apology for not telling you this."

"What is it about him that made you not share him with us? Why didn't you want us to be with you on that day? I would've thought your wedding day was one of the most important days in the world."

Shame ripped apart her gut. It wasn't as if Shai was intentionally making her feel like she was shit at the bottom of her shoe, because her sister would never do that. However, very calm, controlled statements only showed her how upsetting this truly was to her sibling.

"It's not like I am embarrassed by him, or by what we did. It was a spur-of-the-moment decision." She shrugged, unsure of the words to make her sister understand. "I don't know how to explain it."

"How long have you been married to him?"

"A little over five years."

Shai narrowed her gaze and Tara could see the wheels whipping at lightning speed in her head as she calculated the dates and time.

"When you took your trip to celebrate becoming the assistant district attorney."

Reaching for a cookie, Tara nodded. That was exactly what had happened. She bit into the soft, buttery chocolate chip goodness and purred. If Shai weren't her sister, and if she was into women, Tara would keep this woman locked up all day to cook and bake.

"Precisely."

"If I remember correctly you went to Thailand. So, who is he, what does he do now, and as is apparent by your earlier statement that he's here, when the fuck do I get to meet him?"

"His name is Andrew Coleman. Last I knew he was living in Switzerland. To be honest he doesn't do all that much that I'm aware of. He's a baron."

Shai paused in the process of eating a cookie, eyes growing wide as she stared at her sister.

"I'm sorry. Did you just casually put out there that you married a baron?"

Tara twiddled her thumbs and nodded. "I did. It's not like that's why married him."

Shai's gaze twinkled and she waggled her eyebrows. "I'm pretty sure I know why you married him."

Tara choked and waved off any assistance. When she finally got herself back under control she drank some more coffee and put one foot up on the chair to rest her knee against her chin.

"That had a lot to do with it, I won't lie. But it wasn't all. There was something about him when we were together." She shoved a hand through her hair and sighed with the weight of the world on her shoulders. "Just felt right being with him."

"Then why not stay with him? Why pretend it doesn't exist for five years, shut him out of your life and not bring him into ours?"

"He wanted me to go home with him, to Switzerland. I did and that's what extended my stay a little bit. I just didn't tell you I was no longer in Thailand. When we got there he was…different."

Shai leaned forward, resting her arms on the table. Sharp, intelligent eyes focused on her face.

"Different how?"

Tara understood what her sister was asking and right away shook her head. "Not as in I was afraid that he would keep me and I wouldn't be able to come home ever again. That wasn't it, not at all. It was…different. Not quite sure how to explain it. Almost like a guy I met and fell in love with in Thailand wore a suit, and when we got back to Switzerland the suit was exchanged and put on someone else's body."

While her gaze was no less intense, the edge faded from Shai's eyes. Her sister may have been a professor but she was fiercely protective of her family.

"So he was acting like a baron?"

Another shrug. "I don't know, Shai. Until him I'd never met another baron. So possibly, but I can't say for certain. Then he told me it was time for me to move there. It was in that moment I realized I wasn't anything more than a piece of eye candy, property for him to have an add-on to a claim. It's like he never once heard me talk about and show my excitement for becoming one of the youngest ADAs the Quad Cities have ever had. Like all our time talking as we walked along the beaches suddenly meant nothing to him. Like jack shit. He assumed that because he was a baron and he liked it, for the moment anyway, living in Switzerland, that I would drop everything and be at his side. He wouldn't even talk to me about it. So I told him I obviously had to come home first, and then would go from there."

"So once you made it home, you just wiped him away and didn't tell us? Didn't even admit it to yourself?"

"That's precisely what I did. I ran from it because I didn't want to face it. And for whatever reason, he's back. And I've run out of options so I have to face him."

Shai got up from the table. Tara tracked her with her gaze as she fixed herself another cup of coffee. Instead of returning, Shai pivoted and relaxed against the countertop, ankles hooked as her dark purple sequined socks gleamed against the shiny floor.

"I just have one final question for you. Okay that's a lie, but one final one for the moment. I reserve the right to request this witness."

Tara smiled and nodded.

"Do you still love him?"

Dammit. It's one helluva good question.

* * * *

Andrew stared out of the window of his penthouse suite, wearing nothing but the towel around his waist. The day was dark and gloomy, more snow falling. It wasn't that he had a problem with snow — he loved it —

this was because his wife was avoiding him. He'd gotten back to her office earlier today only to be told she was out and they wouldn't tell him when she was coming back.

He never even attempted to play the husband card because he had no doubt she'd not told anybody about them and their marriage. Another fact that hurt.

So he'd been in here all afternoon, finally taking a long hot shower, hoping it would calm him down and relax his tense muscles. So far it hadn't worked, at least not the relaxing, but he was warm and the hotel was passable.

Behind him, in the reflection from the mirror, he could see the steam billowing out from the bathroom. The view he had from the window here didn't quite match his one in Switzerland, but that wasn't a fair comparison, were he to be honest. This was still missing something, as did his one he had at home. If he had his choice, there would be a tiny little woman right beside him—one who went by the title of *his wife*—wrapped in a robe of her own or naked. He was good with either.

He scratched his facial hair, debated shaving it for about five seconds, then shook his head, refusing to entertain that notion further. Spinning on his heel, he made his way to the foot of the king-sized bed and sat.

Andrew bunched his fists and pounded the mattress on either side of his thighs. He just needed one chance. Just one, to get her to reconsider everything from giving him another opportunity to actually being his wife in more than just the name.

His phone rang and he swore as he made his way over to where it sat on the tall dresser. Scowling at his own reflection, he swept it up and answered with a sharp, "What?"

"Just calling to check in as you said you wanted me to do."

He closed his eyes and shook his head at the alto tone of his personal assistant, Wendy Grider. "I'm fairly certain I said I don't need you to check on me, Wendy. I can handle this myself and don't need any of your interference."

Silence lingered between them for a few moments before she cleared her throat.

"Take it as you will. All I know is before I started working for you, you were a mess. I'm here to make your life easier and run much more organized. It would've been a lot simpler had you just let me come over there and bring her back over here."

For one of us maybe.

"I don't even know why I told you about her."

"Again, because I'm your personal assistant. I can't do my job if you're holding out on secrets with me. I'm surprised it took me this long to find out that you actually had a wife. I should've known from the jump, would've made everything so much simpler. Regardless, that is not why I'm calling."

He rubbed his temple. The stirrings of a migraine were raising their ugly head and making themselves known. "Of course it's not. What's going on?"

"There're some issues with a few of your holdings and I need you to look over the proposal I'm sending on the best ways that we can handle this. I've already sent them and here's where I really need you to listen. I need this back in no more than forty-eight hours."

The migraine stopped ebbing at him with the potential of arriving and fully popped out. Wendy was damn good at her job, which was why he'd hired her. But there were times when the woman just didn't take a hint and let things go. This would have been one of those times. This *should* have been one of those times. However, Wendy being who she was, pit bull with a bone, wasn't letting it go.

"I'm not here to work on any proposals, I'm here to bring my wife home."

"How nice. Multitask. Women do it all the time. Besides, your wife is in court for a case and she has another following it, then there's lunch with her sister Shai."

He perked right up. "How do you know my wife's schedule?" How the hell was it that Wendy knew but he didn't?

"Please," she scoffed. "From the moment I learned about her, I've been keeping tabs on her. You paid for her hospital stay after she was shot."

His blood ran ice cold. "What did you say?"

"She was shot a while ago. I told you this and you hemmed and hawed before climbing back on your jet to head off to Dubai for a meeting." Disappointment lined her tone. "I felt you should pay for it as you're still married, so I took care of that and have been keeping tabs on her to make sure she doesn't need anything. I like her, she's smart as a whip."

His jaw tingled and he fought back the urge to hurl. Had he truly been so callous?

Obviously I was, since she didn't think of coming to me for anything, nor did she let me know that happened.

"I'll send back the papers, but right now, I have to speak to my wife." He ended the call before she could say another word. After he tossed the phone onto the mattress, he picked up the pillow, shoved his face in there and screamed in anger.

I have so much to make up for.

He opened the closet and pulled out a suit. Before long he was moving from the hotel lobby to the waiting town car. With a nod to the man holding the door, he slid over the smooth leather seat.

Jaw set, he tugged on the cuff of his suit coat and flicked a dismissive gaze over his attire. This would work.

He read a bit of the paperwork during the ride across the Quad Cities to the courthouse he needed to reach. His anger grew as he realized what Wendy was talking about. Two of his distributors were skimming. This would be handled.

The car slowed and he closed the document as his skin prickled. Soon, he would see her once more.

"I'll call when I'm ready," he said as he moved past the driver.

"Very good, sir." The young man tipped his hat and headed back to the driver's seat.

Andrew strode up the large steps in front of the courthouse. As he entered, he frowned again at the sight of the metal detectors.

Really?

It bothered him to see she had to go through these, here and at her job. He put his money clip, wallet, passport, phone, and change into an ugly gray container, then walked through. The guard there gave him a brief smile but didn't speak.

As he returned all his things, his screen lit up and he swiped it, seeing a message from Wendy. *I owe her a raise.*

She'd texted him the courtroom location. Lengthening his stride, he found the room, ensured his phone was on vibrate and pushed in to sit along the back. A fat man in an expensive suit paced before the jury at the moment, telling them about his client.

Angling his head a bit, he could see the back of his wife's head. All that thick, glorious hair had been wrenched back into a tight bun. He could see only a few strands of the hot pink that had grabbed his attention last night.

She didn't fidget. Her back was ramrod straight and once in a while he saw her make some notes on a pad beside her. He crossed his arms and listened.

He could acknowledge he hadn't paid full attention until the man walked to his seat and Tara rose. She wore the hell out of her dark charcoal-gray suit with thin stripes of pink through it.

One of the things he'd always admired about her from the start was her confidence. She may not have had a lot of physical height but her self-confidence made her appear ten feet tall.

She tugged on the hem of her suitcoat and approached the defendant who sat on the stand. "Mr. Abernathy. I only have a few questions for you, then you can get down." The man shot her a smile, probably thinking she was going to go easy on him.

It wasn't an action she returned. Andrew sat back in the bench and watched as his wife tore into the man and reduced him to a quivering pile of tears.

Chapter Three

Only her professional demeanor kept her expression devoid of anything the moment she laid her gaze upon the man in the back row, staring at her as she did her job in the front.

What the hell is he doing here? Why is he here? And how the hell did he figure out where I am?

Aware her expression didn't give any of her thoughts away, she coolly dismissed him by turning back around. She walked to the front of the table she and her assistant used. Once she'd finished clasping her hands before her, she sighed and turned her attention to the men and women of the jury.

"One final question for you, Mr. Abernathy."

The man wiped the corners of his eyes. Her heart had no feeling for him, nothing in the way of sympathy. He was a bully and an ass of the highest caliber and she despised men—people really—who were like that. Smooth, with money, who thought he could charm his way out of any situation that didn't go well for him.

It was why he'd ignored his attorney's advice. She knew David Sala wouldn't have advised him to take the stand. She'd worked across from that man far too long to know him to do otherwise. So that meant he was confident he could charm her as well as the jury.

It was difficult for her to keep the smug attitude hidden. The tears may have started as fake but as she progressed, she knew they had become real as he realized that this wasn't going at all how he wanted.

Pushing the lingering thoughts of her husband to the back of her mind, she took a deep breath and gave the jury a slight nod of acknowledgment, wanting them to know she understood this was important.

"What exactly did you think should happen when Ms. Hunter said no to you in front of all those potential clients?"

"No one says no to me. She never should have."

Realization hit him and she watched his expression pale. In her peripheral vision she noticed David grind his jaw in frustration.

"Thank you, Mr. Abernathy."

"That's not what I meant to say. You're twisting my words," he hollered. "I never met this woman."

"The prosecution rests, Your Honor."

She walked back to her chair and couldn't help but allow her gaze to sweep the spectators, moving with expedited speed over the family of the victim and along her husband, who'd moved a tiny bit. Another dismissive glance and she sat down beside her co-counsel.

He shared a look with her as the defense counsel tried to redirect, but the damage had already been done.

"Closing arguments tomorrow at nine a.m." The gavel banged down and they all rose as the judge walked out.

She checked her wrist and swore. It was going to be close.

"I have to haul ass to my next court case. I will meet up with you back at the office and we'll finalize the closing."

Okay, so she already had it finished but there were some tweaks she had to put in, given how today had gone.

"I'll be there. I'll bring dinner."

She grinned at Amir Dixon. "I'm looking forward to it. Gotta run, see you later." As she grabbed her briefcase, she shared a look with David as well. The man wanted to meet for a plea.

"Call me, David, I'm due in Mathis' courtroom and I really don't want to be late."

"Count on it." He waved her on and she lengthened her stride toward the door.

All the lawyers knew Judge Mathis and she wasn't one anyone wanted to get on the bad side of. It was on the other end of the court building and two levels up.

Some days it sucks having short legs.

He fell into step beside her and she refused to listen to her body's need to sway in his direction. As he kept pace with her without any strain on his part, she waited for him to speak. It wasn't until they hit the stairwell that he did.

"We need to talk."

"Now's not going to happen, Drew. I'm busy."

"It's Andrew."

"Whatever."

She hustled up the stairs, grateful for Shai dragging her along to all those butt-fuck early ass spin classes, so she wasn't going to be looking like a fish out of water as she stood before the judge.

"Why do you have to make everything so damn difficult?"

She ground her jaw and prayed for patience. It wouldn't do not only to miss her court appointment but also have to be bailed out of jail because her temper had gotten the best of her.

"Why are you so determined to try and reduce everything anyone else does to nothing if it inconveniences you? Newsflash, I'm in the middle of my work day. I'm not stopping to fuel your need to absolute supremacy. It's not going to happen."

He grabbed her upper arm, swinging her around so they were face-to-face.

Her brain short-circuited. That could prove to be problematic. This man was her weakness—her Achilles' heel, so to speak. Those incredible eyes stared down at her from beneath his thick lashes.

This, right here, this is why I moved away from him. Because it was about him and he makes me lose my train of thought.

His grip softened. Not enough for her to pull free, but so he wouldn't leave a mark, yet she couldn't help but feel his touch all the way to her clit. "I know you're working, just like I know you are going to see your sister later. But *we* need to talk. I need to know what the hell is going on here. Oh, and about you being shot."

"Stalkerish much?"

His eyes hardened as they narrowed. "When it comes to my wife? Hell no. Five years, Tara."

"Oh, lookie, the baron can count. Good for you. Here's another number. Two. That's how many minutes I have until I'm held in contempt of court. So let go of my arm." This time she yanked back from him, an immediate curse escaping in regards to the emptiness within her as well as the rebellious cells who gravitated back toward him.

Shoving away all warm fuzzy thoughts, she hauled ass for the door and slipped inside with fifteen seconds to spare. She didn't delude herself into thinking that this was over between them, not by a long shot.

Think on it later – right now, we have a case to win.

After that finished, along with a call to Shai to push back their lunch, she was with Amir in her office, takeout between them as they finished up everything she needed to do prior to closing arguments tomorrow morning.

"You have a visitor, Ms. Monroe."

"Send them in, Marvin," she replied without looking up from the papers.

"Tara."

The fork in her hand wobbled as Andrew's molten voice poured over her, much like the warm chocolate he used to drizzle on her prior to licking it off. Or was that the honey, syrup and more? Her nipples pushed against the sateen of her bra and she fought the urge to squeeze her legs together.

Lifting her head, she couldn't help but notice the silent question in Amir's gaze.

"Coleman," she returned. "What are you doing here?"

"We need to talk."

Her blood simmered. "Like I told you earlier, I'm busy. I don't change my schedule merely because you saunter into town."

"I'm not leaving, Tara. You can't ignore me forever." Challenge dangled from his lips with those words.

"I can have you banned from ever coming in here."

One eyebrow rose and a dangerous, warning glint filled his gaze. "Is that how you want to play this?"

She knew she should back down. But this man, damn it all, got beneath her skin in so many ways.

"I'm not playing." She nodded to Marvin.

"Yes, ma'am, Ms. Monroe. Sir, you need to come with me."

Andrew stood up and his gaze flashed with lightning. "Very well, Mrs. Coleman. I'll be back once the papers hear of their ADA who's married to a baron."

She closed her eyes as those words fled his lips. Amir's and Marvin's gazes bored into her. She didn't look away from Andrew.

"The name is Ms. Monroe," she ground out.

"I don't think so. I've never been served with divorce papers and I'm damn sure we fucking consummated the *hell* out of our marriage, so no way it was annulled." He tugged on one sleeve of his perfect-fit coat. "So, Baroness Coleman, when will you have time to speak to your husband? Now? Or should I go to the news?"

If only this plastic fork were a steak knife, I'd put it right between his ribs.

Andrew had her, he knew this. That announcement alone had done it, but at the same time, he couldn't help but wonder if he'd not just lost her all the same. Her incredible black eyes raged hot, then nothing. Not anger, suspicion, or desire for revenge.

Blank.

And with Tara that was never a good thing.

Damn it, if she'd not pushed the issue. The other two men looked between themselves.

"Ms. Monroe?" the guard asked.

Andrew bristled. That *wasn't* her name. Tara held up a finger and put her fork on the plate. A move he was grateful for, unsure she wouldn't try to take out an eye with it. She moved toward him until they were millimeters from each other.

"You will leave with Marvin and wait in his office until I get there. You won't talk to him or annoy him, or so help me, I'll rid this world of a baron and make myself a widow."

She vibrated with the force of her anger.

"Then?" he pushed, because he wanted her to know he wasn't a man to lie there and take this behavior.

"We talk and you get the fuck out of my life." She whirled around and went back to her seat. As she sat, she glared at him, then her gaze softened as she looked to Marvin, who escorted him out.

Another hour passed before something told him to look up. He saw her walking down the hall toward the office. Her eyes were closed and she was rubbing the back of her neck.

He hated seeing her like this, exhausted and stressed. *If she'd just let me take care of her.*

"Move," she barked at him.

He got up as she went to Marvin and bent down to whisper in his ear, then she turned and walked away. Hastening after her, he caught up and cleared his throat when she didn't speak.

"Not a single word out of you until we're out of this building, Drew."

Clamping back his retort, he held the door for her as she pushed past him into the cold night.

"Am I allowed to talk now?"

"Where did you park?" She snorted. "Where did you have your man park your car?"

There was no denying the derision in her words.

"I had him drop me off."

"Just my fucking luck," she muttered. "Where are you staying?"

He gave her the name of his hotel and she swore again before striking off, heading down the steps at a rapid speed. Andrew hurried after her. She stopped next to a SUV and when he just stood there, she looked at him, disgust all over her face.

"You actually have to get in yourself. I'm not holding the door for you." Rolling her eyes, she hopped behind the wheel while he climbed into the passenger side.

The moment his belt was buckled, they were pulling out of her parking spot. The interior smelled like cherry blossom and he hid a smile. She smelled like them and no doubt had some air freshener to keep it around her. They were, after all, her favorite flower.

"Talk—you have until we get to the hotel."

"No way, Tara. You owe me more than that."

"I owe you?"

Her voice, low and dangerous, flowed over him.

"Yes. For fuck's sake, we're married. You owe me the decency of a face to face without a time limit to talk about this."

"For the record, I owe you shit, but fine, let's deal with this now." She cleared her throat and said, "Call Shai."

"Where are you and how long before you get here?" A low cultured voice reached out from the speakers.

"I've got my husband in the car and apparently I *owe* him a face-to-face."

Andrew waited for her to sneer along with Tara.

"You do," Shai said, her voice even keel.

Okay, even he was shocked by that. And from the screech Tara released, she was as well.

"Excuse me? How are you siding with him? I'm your sister."

"You were the one who married him, Tara. Not the rest of us. Hell, we didn't even know you were married.

As it is, I'm still the only one in the family who does, unless you've come clean to them since we last spoke?" A momentary pause. "Didn't think so."

"I hate you," she grumbled, and Andrew wasn't sure just who the words were for.

"That's okay, I'll still love you when you get over yourself. As I was pointing out. You married him. If you want to divorce him, fine, we'll support that, but you do owe him a face-to-face. Unless you're telling me he was abusive?" Ice lined the question.

"No," Tara replied without hesitation, soothing the unease that sprang up within him. "He never did anything like that."

"So there's no danger. Spend time with him, fuck him again if you must, get it out of your system then divorce him."

"Christ, Shai, you do know he's in the vehicle with me, right?"

"You say that like I should care. I wasn't good enough to be introduced to him. Come by when you're done with him."

She was gone.

Cutting his gaze to the woman driving, he saw the exhaustion on her features. "Is she expecting you tonight?"

"Knowing Shai, yes." She pulled into the parking lot of his hotel and killed the engine.

Her reluctance poured from her. Andrew hated this. He undid his belt and got out. Moving to her door before she could get out, he blocked her in with his larger form.

"This isn't a death sentence, Tara. I promise."

His hands burned with the need to touch her once more. Allow himself the privilege of pushing into that thick, glossy hair of hers. Feel it sliding over his skin, holding it close to his nose and inhaling the subtle scent of cherry blossom and white sandalwood.

Instead of touching her, he backed off, holding the door as she climbed out. Once she'd locked her vehicle, he offered his arm and noted the reluctance she had to take it. Or was that her reluctance to touch him?

Either way, he wasn't pleased. His anger was soothed the moment she rested her hand upon the sleeve of his coat. Together they entered the hotel, strode for the elevator and rode up to his penthouse suite.

His mind raced with the possibility of stripping her bare of all her clothing.

It was so long since she'd been naked beneath him, since his cock had slipped inside her and been surrounded by her scorching heat.

Chapter Four

Tara gazed around as she entered the suite. Her palm still burned from where she'd had it upon his arm. Even with the leather between them, she had no recourse from the heat emanating from him. Out of instinct, she drifted her gaze to the open doorway leading to the bedroom. No, not *the* bedroom, *his*. She fought to hide her flush when he turned with a complete arrogant smirk on his face.

Bastard.

Damn if he didn't make it hot.

"I'm here. Speak your piece."

The longer I'm around him, the weaker I will become.

Anger and irritation flared in his eyes before he reined them in. He shrugged out of his black leather jacket only to drape it over the back of a chair. Her mouth dried as he shoved the sleeves of his shirt up, allowing her to see the muscular forearms.

"That's not how this will go, Tara." His voice held an edge. "You will remove your coat, sit, and share a drink while we speak."

She narrowed her eyes. "You don't call the shots."

One dark eyebrow rose as he poured two drinks from the mini bar. "I beg to differ." He gestured with one hand. "Sit."

Leaving her coat on, part defiance, part necessary armor, she moved to a chair and sat.

He neared and handed her a drink. She took it only to set it beside her. Not drinking and driving was something she was serious about and she had no intention of being here long enough for any drink to wear off—there was no reason for her to begin to indulge.

Drew lowered himself across from her and crossed his legs. She never thought of him as Andrew. He'd introduced himself as Drew that first afternoon they'd met on the beach and that was the man she'd fallen in love with. Not the one who wore the mantle of Baron Andrew Coleman.

Skimming her tongue along her teeth, she waited. This, *this* was a game she excelled at. Tara steepled her fingers and watched the man she'd married.

He held her gaze as he put the amber liquid up to his lips and drank. She didn't blink as he swallowed.

"You're not drinking."

"And you're not talking."

"We're not divorcing."

"Fine. Good talk. We go back to how things were." She flicked a hand along her pantsuit. "Anything else?"

When he remained silent, she began to rise and he narrowed those blue eyes once more. With a huff, she sat back and crossed her ankles.

"Get on with it then."

"Why are you rushing to get away from me? We've not seen each other for five years and you have somewhere else to be?"

She rolled her eyes, exasperated. "This isn't all about you."

"That's right," he ground out. "It's all about you and what you want." The sarcasm drenching the words raised her ire.

"I suppose it is. I mean I married a man I barely knew, and a week after we tie the knot, I swear it was like looking at the shell of the same man, but he was entirely different. An ass, uncaring of what I wanted, what I wished for, my dreams and aspirations."

He leaned back against the chair as if she'd delivered a full-on physical slap to him, eyes wide and shocked.

"Is that what you think? What you thought? That I didn't care about your dreams?" He cleared his throat. "That I *don't* care?"

"Why wouldn't I think that? After we were wed, it was all about you and how there were things to attend. How we would be overseas from my family, how I would be with you every step of the way."

He moved his cup to the table beside him where his strong fingers lingered on the glass, moving along the rim.

"You are my wife."

"Then why even pretend to listen to what I said on those walks, you know, the few times you acted, at least, like you cared what I said? You invented interest in me. But for the life of me, I can't imagine why. I'm not exactly 'baroness' material. I wouldn't expect a tiny Asian woman to be what a baron would pick."

He flexed his jaw.

"Are you finished?"

Aliyah Burke

She needed her sister's ear. "I believe I am. And while this has been spectacular for me to catch up, I should be going." Getting to her feet, she then made her way to the door. The second she closed her fingers around the latch, he was there.

Drew had her up against the firm barrier of the door. Every hard inch of him held her there. She closed her eyes and sucked in a deep breath. While the air was important, it was both necessary and a curse the moment his masculine scent filled her nose, shooting need and raw lust through her.

The long, thick length of his cock was blatant against her and she licked her lips, trying to stem the flow of moisture gathering between her legs. A whimper slipped free as he nuzzled the side of her neck.

"If this is what you've believed for all these years, I've seriously neglected my job as your husband. A fact I must tell you, I am fully anticipating the fun I will have making you realize just how wrong you were."

It had been so long since she'd been this close to a man. Her man. Damn it, all she wanted to do was sink back into him and let herself indulge.

"It's fact, Drew. And the fact that you think otherwise is just more proof."

Her phone rang and it took a moment to dig it from her pants pocket. Not making him move back, his warmth was fucking amazing.

"Yes?"

Great, my voice is all deep and husky.

"I had a question because I was thinking."

Shai.

Tara cleared her throat. Behind her, Drew kissed along the nape of her neck.

"About?"

"If you were married when we all went off on our Mexican week of hard sex and fun in the sun, what did you do?"

Drew stilled behind her, one large hand wrapped around her small waist, anchoring them together. The graze of his teeth could be felt along the same path his lips had just taken.

"Now isn't the best time to talk about that, Shai." Heat flushed through her entire body.

"Why not? You're the one who said sometimes you just need cock. Oh, you are still with him then. I will just eat my dinner alone. Do you think you'll be by for dessert? You know, you could bring your husband and I can meet him. I think that's a good plan."

"Shai."

"Well, get the fucking done with and come on."

"I think it's a great idea," Drew said loud enough she knew Shai could hear.

Of course he would.

"Excellent. I will see you soon." She hung up.

He took the phone from her hand and threw it behind them somewhere. She honestly didn't care.

"What's this about you going to Mexico for a time with some man?"

"That's not pertinent to this discussion."

He bumped his hips into her. "You, my beautiful wife, have never been so wrong."

"We should just get a divorce, Drew. You go on your way and I'll go on mine."

"No."

Not a lot of ways to misinterpret that single statement.

"I didn't chase you down across the world to have a divorce, Tara. I came because I want my wife."

She bit the inside of her lip. "I'm sure there are any number of women who would love to be a baroness. Marry one of them."

He spun her so they were face-to-face. She'd always been so tiny and petite next to him and had loved it. Loved how he made her feel so protected, feminine, sexy.

Right now, however, she was at a disadvantage and she didn't like it one bit. He wasn't stupid and knew how to read her reactions to him, knew she was lusting after him.

"Is that what you want? A divorce so you can trot back to Mexico and hook up with whomever you slept with down there?"

He gripped her chin and forced her head back to maintain eye contact. She gulped.

"Is it?" Those two words rumbled from his throat as fire burned in his gaze.

Andrew seethed. The thought of another man laying a single finger on her enraged him. He forced himself to release her, because he would never cause her physical harm.

Even so, staring down at her, he was lost in her deep eyes.

"I spent a week at a spa, getting massages and sleeping. Nothing more. I've not betrayed the vows I took."

He searched her features for a lie but didn't see any. He settled the back of his hand alongside her face.

"But your sisters think you were with a man? Because, sometimes you just need dick?"

His own pulsed and he bit the inside of his lower lip so he didn't thrust against her. He could read her like a book, even after all this time, and knew without a doubt she was aroused.

"We were speaking for Eva." The corner of her lips twitched.

Andrew had always had a fascination with her mouth. Her lips were like a delectable candy he wanted to indulge in. They were an erogenous zone for her. Had they changed or did she still crinkle her nose at the brush against the back of her knees? Did kisses along her ankle have her panting in need?

"Well, I think you do need cock. It's been far too long for either of us."

She arched a perfect eyebrow. "Really? How long has it been since you've had a nice, thick cock?"

He gripped her chin. "You know that's not what I meant."

A heavy sigh. "I'm not sleeping with you, Drew. You wanted to talk, so talk. I have places to go."

"We have places to go. We shouldn't keep Shai waiting — let me change and we will head out." Before she could say anything, he kissed her.

Fuck!

The contact was too goddamn fucking brief, rocking him to the core, but he backed away and headed to his bedroom to change into something a bit less stuffy. He had to make a good impression on her sister.

Not trusting her to wait if he took a long time, he shoved himself into jeans and a dark blue Henley. Hiking boots on his feet, he swiped his identification and key card before making his way back out to the living area. She remained by the door, still wearing her coat and not having drunk a drop.

"Ready."

She flicked her gaze over him before spinning around and exiting the room. Grabbing his jacket, he hurried after her, catching up at the elevator. He stepped in and pinned her with his gaze. Hers didn't waver and he bit back some concern.

This woman wasn't the same one he'd married. Then again, perhaps she was and now she'd just come into her own. He didn't know much about her, if he were to be honest to himself about it, because he had been focused on winning her.

Her warning words flicked through his mind. She was right. He hadn't really thought much about what she wanted once she'd married him. It had all been about him.

At her car, he held the door for her, ignored her suspicious look and just made his way to the passenger side once she was securely in. While he preferred to drive, he didn't have a clue where Shai lived, so he wouldn't push that particular boat.

Tara didn't move the vehicle until he buckled up. Snow had begun to fall again in earnest and he couldn't help but admire the way she handled the drive. The music was low and as they cruised along, he tried to compare this woman to the one he'd first met.

Still a spitfire, yet *more*.

After a full twenty minutes of silence, one she never asked him to break, she slowed in a neighborhood before pulling up to a modest house.

Andrew climbed out and, as he rounded the hood, the front door opened. As he helped Tara out, he watched a woman step from the house. His wife led the way and paused at the bottom of the steps before she looked up.

"Shai, Drew. Drew, Shai."

Tara slipped past her and into the house, leaving him alone with the black woman who watched him like a mama bear protecting a cub. *Her* cub.

Why am I fearing this? I've done countless deals that have made me nervous. This is one woman.

Even as he moved closer, he knew the answer — because she was Tara's sister. "Andrew Coleman."

"And am I to call you Drew or Andrew?"

"Andrew."

"I see. Drew is the private name between you. Short like the sex you had if you're here so soon. Now I understand her frustration."

What the fuck?

"We didn't have sex."

She turned her back on him and went to the door. "Come on in, food's waiting."

Andrew trailed her in and closed the thick door behind him. The rich, mouthwatering scent of food permeated the air and his belly growled in anticipation.

"Don't feel bad, her cooking has that effect on people."

Tara moved past him from the living room to the open kitchen where Shai stood over the stovetop, light shining off the violet in her hair. Two stunning women stood there and he knew deep in his gut he was a lucky bastard to have one of them in his life.

Now I have to find a way to keep her there.

"Come on in. Get a drink and pull up a stool."

Obeying, he noticed how much more relaxed Tara was now.

"Thank you." He poured himself a glass of white wine.

Shai shrugged. "I love to cook."

Silence reigned for all of two minutes. Shai glanced between them both. "Someone should start talking."

From the mutinous set of Tara's lush mouth, it wasn't going to be her.

"What do you do, Ms. Monroe?"

"Shai, please. I'm a professor and unless you love math, you will find it boring. I want to know how you two met."

His gaze shot to Tara and heat filled him when he found she was already watching him. He gave a gentle smile.

"That's easy. It was a Thursday afternoon and I was walking along a beach on Ko Pha Ngan when I spied her near Sunrise Beach. She was playing in the surf with some of the local kids."

The corners of Tara's mouth turned up as a faint flush danced over her olive skin. It was the first hint of shyness since he'd been reunited with her.

"Always did love kids, this one."

With deft motions, Tara portioned up equal amounts of food onto the plates Shai had set before her.

"Stop acting like you don't." Tara paused to shoot her sister a glare without all that much heat to it.

Shai ignored her, instead gesturing at him in a way he took to mean *carry on*. Then she slid a dark cranberry-hued plate before him, piled with stuffed ravioli, green beans and some hot, buttery dinner rolls — the kind with the three sections that could be torn into with ease.

"Mushroom and chicken stuffed ravioli, a dried tomato pesto sauce, green beans. Are you allergic?"

Now she asks me this after *setting this plate before me smelling like manna from heaven? Who cares? I'm eating it.*

"Don't believe so."

"Good, the doc isn't here to save your life. I mean, I could try a tracheotomy but I'm not sure—"

"I'll be fine, thank you. Smells amazing."

Tara had already begun to eat, apparently not waiting on them to finish discussing if he would need her sister to cut open his neck so he could breathe later if he ate with them.

"How long after you met were you in bed together?"

Andrew gestured to Tara. "I'll let you answer this one since I got the first one."

"Ass," she muttered, not so quiet.

"A nice one from what I saw as he walked to the driver's door." Shai cut up each square into smaller pieces before eating them. Completely different from Tara, who stabbed and ate.

Andrew flushed yet winked at Tara when their eyes locked once more.

As the food and wine went on, Andrew realized how much they loved and respected each other. He liked Shai even if—according to her—she had yet to make her mind up on him.

He helped clean up after the meal, then they switched locations from the warm kitchen to the living room. With the fire roaring inside, the snow falling outside and his wife beside him, Andrew didn't want to be anywhere else.

Tara excused herself and vanished down the hall.

"Thank you again for the meal, it was delicious."

She watched him unwaveringly. "Why do you want back in her life?"

The question was expected and yet he didn't want to respond. That was between him and Tara at the end of it all.

"Don't want to tell me, fine. Heed me well, *Baron*, I'm fucking" — she rose and stood before him — "sick of men hurting my sisters. Really fucking annoyed by it. I maybe the youngest, but I'm definitely not the nicest of us."

"Everything okay?"

"Fine," he replied as Tara entered the room.

"Merely taking his drink for a refill." Shia's brown eyes bore into him as she plucked his glass away.

Andrew opened his mouth when his phone rang. A tone only one person in this world had.

"What, Wendy?"

Both women focused on him with laser intensity.

Shit.

Chapter Five

Tara's gut churned at the sound of another woman's name rolling off his tongue with such familiar ease. She wasn't an unknown, because she had Drew's number.

I don't have that.

Not necessarily true. If he had the same number from years ago, she had it in her phone. Where it had sat for the past few years under BAC. That was it.

Not that it mattered now. It was apparent he had a woman in his life named Wendy. Shai didn't stick around but went to the kitchen where she opened another bottle of wine.

"Either confront him about it or let it go."

"What?" She gripped the wineglass so hard, she was shocked it didn't break.

"I'm not an idiot, Tara. Both of us thought the same thing when he answered his phone like that. You're either going to confront him or let it go."

Draining the newly filled glass of wine, she stared at her sister. "Why the fuck would I let it go?"

"Because you've let him go for the past five years. Not caring what or *who* he did."

That hurt.

"Not true," she protested.

Shai didn't blink as they stood there, gazes locked. Tara cursed her sister in every way she knew how. Unperturbed, Shai took it.

She blinked once after Tara's tirade finished. "Done?"

Angry tears burned the backs of her eyes and she nodded, refusing to allow them to spill free.

"You're cold at times, Shai."

"No, I'm pragmatic. You can't be mad at him for something you've not given a damn about for the past few years. Especially when you don't know what it's about." Her brown gaze softened. "This tells me how much you still care for him, because the kick ass lawyer you are knows that you need more than circumstantial evidence."

"What are you saying?"

Shai moved closer to her and held her hands, tight. "I am saying that there was a reason you didn't divorce him. You watch him like a starving woman who can't get enough of the feast before her. What did we tell Eva?"

"That she had to face him and then decide, even though we know she's still in love with Grant."

Shai lifted an eyebrow. "And if she were here, you know damn well she'd be on my side about this. I'm going to bed. You two stay and talk. If you don't want him to stay, send him on his way. Or go with him. Either way, talk." She kissed Tara's cheek and swept out of the kitchen like a royal. Before she got down the hall, she paused and turned back. "Before I forget, Mom and Dad are coming for breakfast so if you don't want them to know about your baron, I would suggest not being here after six."

Alone, she watched Drew as he talked to this Wendy person. Unreasonable jealousy almost overwhelmed her. Giving in, she stomped over to him and glared.

"I told you I would have them to you, why are you calling now?" He lifted his head and speared her with the deep blue of his eyes. "Wait a minute." Drew covered the phone with his hand. "Are we leaving?"

The way he said *we* nearly weakened her resolve. "I am. If you want a ride back to your hotel, come on. If you want to crash here, fine." She pivoted on her feet and got two steps before he stopped her.

"I'll call you back, Wendy." She sneered, slapping her mask back into place before he spun her back to face him. "What is your problem? Why can't you allow me to walk beside you and assist you with your coat as a gentleman should?"

"Why don't you finish your call to Wendy and I'll be outside?"

"She's fine. I'll call her back." He pushed his phone into his jeans pocket.

"Isn't she going to wonder why you have to call her back?"

"No, why would she? She knows I'm here with you."

That jealousy wouldn't leave her alone—it just sat there and nipped at her heels.

"And she's fine with you out trying to get into another woman's pants?" Her words were clipped and short.

His confusion melted away into understanding. "You're jealous."

"Am not," she protested.

He helped her into her coat and led her to the car. "Take me back to the hotel."

She stewed the entire ride, wanting him to explain, but he did no such thing. He didn't say a single word as they drove along the snowy roads. Her own anger grew with each passing mile and each falling snowflake. Still, he was silent.

At the hotel, she slammed on the brakes before the front door. "There you go."

"You're coming with me."

Four words issued with complete confidence.

"Why would I do that?"

He turned toward her in the faint light. There wasn't any softness about him and her pussy spasmed at the heat and determination on his features.

"Don't make this any harder, Tara. We're about to have our talk now. Then…"

"Then what?"

"Then I'm fucking my wife. Park the goddamn car and let's go up to the suite."

Her nipples beaded and pressed against the smoothness of her bra. Pretty damn sure there would be a wet spot on the seat when she got up, she followed his order and parked. He was there to help her out and this time, he slipped an arm around her, leading her to the door.

Tension was taut between them as they crossed the lobby floor and rode up in the elevator. She didn't say a word, even though she did wonder if anyone had recognized her. She would hope not.

"Let's try this again," he stated when they made it inside his room. "Coat off. Ass in chair. Because I'll be damned if you're leaving again tonight."

She watched him yank off his leather jacket and toss it onto a chair. Tara removed hers a bit slower, but his sharp gaze didn't let her refuse. He gestured to her drink and while she didn't need any more alcohol in her system, she did reclaim the chair she'd been in the first time she was here.

"Let's get this out in the open and over so we can move on. Wendy is my personal assistant."

She snorted. "Is that what you're calling it?"

He glared.

"She's been with me for four years now. I've not fucked her a single time, nor have I ever even tried to elicit sexual favors from her. She works for me and no, she wouldn't have a problem with me being here with you, aside from the fact she thought she should have come to get you because I have a hostile takeover going on in one of my holdings I should be dealing with. She's known you were my wife for a long time. She is the one who paid for your medical bills after you were shot. *Another* thing we will be discussing."

"Easy to say."

He shoved a hand through his hair. His eyes and face were hard, an unreadable mask.

"I don't lie. If I say I didn't sleep with her then, goddammit, Tara, I didn't. I'm married. And as I'm taking you at your word that you didn't betray our vows, I'm telling you neither have I. Jesus, woman, I don't want anyone else but you. Haven't since that first moment I laid eyes on you."

Words that melted her—yet, if that were the case, why hadn't he come sooner? She bit the inside of her cheek, hard enough to draw blood and re-center her focus on not falling into a small pile of mush, just because this man turned on the charm.

I'm not falling for it. I won't. He has been charming to get what he wanted, me as a wife. Then he changed.

Even so, Shai's words echoed in her head and she wasn't sure what to do anymore. It was hell being this close to him and not being able to touch him, be held by him.

"Words," she said. "I hear pretty speeches all the time and, like I tell them, actions speak louder than words."

"Enough," he snapped, rocketing up from the chair.

His entire body quivered with leashed power that barely seemed capable of holding him back.

Those deep blue eyes of his were so dark they would have passed as black. He prowled toward her, the beast released him from his shackles. Yet, she couldn't move. She had grown roots despite the quaking her insides were doing. No denying it, there was more than a bit of fear there — he was imposing as shit.

Andrew didn't slow, just stalked up to her, eyes locked on her the entire way. He shoved his hands deep into her hair, anchoring her there — not that she would have been able to move — and slammed his mouth over hers.

This wasn't anything like the kiss he'd given her earlier in the night when they'd first arrived there. No. Not even close.

Primal.

Proprietary.

She erupted in flames and whimpered as her legs wobbled with their pathetic attempt to hold her upright.

Does he kiss Wendy like this? Or someone else?

Iced water sluiced down her face and she tried to pull back. He didn't let her. She bit at his tongue and he broke off the kiss, glaring down at her. One second, two, three. Drew growled low in his throat and shook his head before tossing her over his shoulder like she weighed nothing. Which, in retrospect she really didn't weigh all that much.

"Drew," she screeched. "Put me down. Damn it, I'm the fucking ADA, you can't do this to me."

He kicked the door to his bedroom open and deposited her on the floor. Tara shook from the combination of excitement, arousal and anger.

"It's Andrew." The words were bit off and his look turned deadlier, if that were possible.

"What the fuck ever," she retorted. "Move. I'm done with this."

"No."

He moved to slam the door behind him, reminding her that she was now alone in a room with a bed and the man she'd not had sex with in five years. A man she dreamed about all the time and hell, had even named her vibrator after. Baron. How pathetic was she for that?

"No?"

"So you can hear. Did you not hear me say that Wendy—"

Crack.

She slapped him across the face as hard as she could manage.

Fuck! That hurt. Tara had a hell of a swing. Andrew stared down at the woman who'd just smacked him. He snarled and pushed her back against the nearest wall, pinning her hands above her head with one of his own.

"What the fuck was that for?"

"I don't want to hear you speak about your slut."

Allowing his left hand to slide along the curve of her hip, he gripped hard, digging his fingers into the flesh.

"Let me go, Drew, or by God, I swear I will—"

Enough was enough.

He dipped his head and possessed her mouth until she had no choice but to submit. The second she did, he felt the change within her. He closed his eyes as she dry humped his thigh, moans, sweet as summer, rolling from her mouth.

He palmed her ass and lifted her, allowing his rigid cock to settle between her legs where it belonged. Where *he* belonged.

No more fighting. No more words, not right now. Pinning her between him and the wall with his body, he used his hands and ripped open her shirt, tiny buttons scattering all over. He didn't give a fuck.

His cock pulsed in his pants and he bucked against her. She had her head against the wall, eyes dilated with passion as she panted, lips swollen from the bruising kisses. Lowering his gaze, he moved it over her pale pink lace strapless bra. She moved her hands from above her head until he pinned a look at her. She put them back.

Just in case, he held them there once more and undid her front clasp with expedition. He jerked his dick a few more times as he stared at her breasts. Fuck, he loved them. She wasn't the biggest but what she had fit perfectly in his hands, nary a wasted inch.

Her nipples tightened and he raked his gaze over her once more before ducking his head and wrapping his lips around one. Her mewl crescendoed into a cry as she bucked against him. He sucked harder as he rasped over the tip with his teeth and tongue.

Andrew paid homage to her other breast before he slammed his mouth back over hers once more, thrusting his tongue deep. Releasing her wrists, he placed both his hands on her breasts, lifting them, tugging on the nipples, rolling them.

He eagerly ate every whimper that came from her mouth, and when her fingers sank into his hair, yanking hard, he stopped kissing her and drew back to stare. Both of them were flushed, panting hard.

Eyes locked on hers, he reached one hand up under the skirt she wore and brushed it along her pussy and the soaked panties blocking her entrance. He tucked a finger along the edge and ran up and down the material, allowing only slight brushes against her. Her mouth fell open as her pants grew shorter and sharper. Her hips bucked and tried to initiate more contact.

His brain short-circuited when she dug her nails into the back of his head along his hairline. That had always been one of his *spots*.

One-handed, he unbuttoned his jeans, shoved them down to around his knees and watched the hunger overflow in her eyes as she focused on his bobbing dick. He gripped himself and said, "Move your panties to the side."

She listened and he lined up the large swollen head with the one place it belonged in this world. Andrew pushed in, not hard, just with a single continuous stroke. She'd been small and tight since he'd first fucked her, but if she'd been without anyone for years, the last thing he wanted to do was hurt her.

"Christ," he gasped. His eyes flickered and his balls had already drawn up, ready to release their seed deep inside her. Nothing he recalled could have come close to this.

"This doesn't change a damn thing," she growled, flexing her muscles around his cock.

His anger spiked along with his need for her. "You're my wife," he rumbled.

"Same as I've been this entire time. Still not changing anything."

He drew back then surged forward. Tara yelled, back arching as she came hard around him.

"Look at me while I fuck you," he commanded.

Her eyes were hazy as she listened to him, lips parted, allowing her pants to escape.

"You're my wife, Tara Lynne Monroe Coleman. *Mine*."

Her nails scraped again and pushed him over the edge of whatever reason he had. Andrew scooped his hands under her ass and powered into her. Relentless. Unyielding. His strokes shook the walls and she was with him the entire time, taking him, working him and asking for more.

For the second time that night, words weren't needed. The room filled with the sounds and scent of sex and desperation. Andrew wasn't a gentle lover. He was rough but his woman gave as good as she got. Over and over he had her creaming on his cock while he continued to thrust hard and deep, using the unforgiving wall to provide additional purchase.

"Drew!" she cried, her velvet walls gripping him in a way they hadn't before.

He couldn't hold out any longer and with a rasped sob, he erupted within her, jets of his release as deep as they could go as they shuddered together. Head on the wall, he sucked in large breaths of air, trying to regain control of his breathing. The woman holding on to him as is she never wanted to let him go, did the same thing.

"Tara, I love you," he muttered in Romansh. The one language he knew she didn't speak. Or at least she hadn't when they'd married.

Unwilling to separate from her, but not positive he wouldn't fall to the floor from the orgasm that had torn through him like a twister, he carried her to the bed and crawled in, still buried deep inside her.

This, this was the woman he remembered. Passion-haze surrounding her, pliant and sexy.

He dipped his head and kissed her once more, the anger gone this time, leaving behind only the tenderness. When she rolled her tongue along his, his cock twitched and thickened once more.

"I'm not even close to being done with you."

He woke later, sated and with a sore back. He would wear her nail marks with pride. Something was missing and that was the woman in bed with him. He reached out, flicked on the light and sat up. The bathroom door was closed and he didn't hear the shower running, so he swung his legs over the side of the bed.

"Tara?" he called out to her.

Silence met him. Andrew rubbed his eyes and found the clock still on the floor where a particularly rowdy session of sex had knocked it off. Four twenty-seven.

A weight settled on his chest and he rubbed his palm over his heart. *She wouldn't, would she?*

Even as he jumped up from the bed, he knew the answer — of course she would. She was Tara. By the time he hit the light for the living area of the suite, he knew she had gone.

Even the buttons of her shirt were no longer on the floor. *And I still don't know where she lives.*

He rooted for his phone and called Wendy.

"Morning, boss."

"Find my wife," he snapped.

"Me? I'm fine, thank you for asking."

He ground his jaw and took several deep breaths. "Morning, Wendy. Where is my wife today?"

"It's nearly four thirty in the morning, I would hope sleeping." She cleared her throat. "Which coincidentally would have given you time to finish going over the documents and get them back to me."

Ignoring the reprimand in her tone, he pivoted to the bathroom and turned on the shower.

"Wendy," he warned as he stared at his reflection.

"You do realize I'm across the world from you right now? Not sure where your wife is. I didn't put a tracker on her. I mean, we could use her phone, but I think that would be crossing the stalkerish line just a bit, even for you."

"Wendy." The growl got deeper.

Steam began billowing out of the large shower. A place he'd enjoyed Tara's body more than once last night and into this morning.

"I'll see what I can do from *Switzerland*, bossman, about your wife in *America*. You know, where you are." She was gone.

Phone on the counter, he stepped beneath the hot spray and took one of the quickest showers he'd ever managed. Giving Wendy until he dried off and dressed, he picked up his phone once more when it rang with her personalized ringtone.

"Talk to me," he said as soon as he answered.

"Your wife is a workaholic. She's got a huge caseload for the rest of the week. So she'll be in her office or at court. With the occasional need to eat and take a piss, that's most likely where you will find her."

"One more thing, Wendy."

"Really? Just one? I live for the challenge. Also, I want those papers back from you within three hours."

"Fine." He stared at the hand that hadn't worn his wedding ring in far too long. "Two actually. I want her home address and my ring sent over."

"Thank God you're not asking me for anything big. I want to tell you, I don't get paid nearly enough for this. I'll have the information ready to send you, after you return the papers." She hung up.

"Manipulated by my own personal assistant." He went to his computer, opened the Mac and pulled up what he needed to read over. He may have been the boss, but Wendy wasn't playing. He wouldn't have a damn thing on Tara, or his ring, if he didn't send the things back to Wendy as she'd ordered.

He put in an order for room service and sat down to get to work. Tara would be next on the list.

Chapter Six

Tara sat wrapped in a crocheted blanket her mother had made for her when she'd first landed the job she had now. Assistant District Attorney. All the lights in her place were off, and she was using the city lights softened by the still-falling snow for illumination.

To her left sat an untouched mug of coffee. Beside her right thigh was her cell phone, face down on the cushion. She could reach anyone in her family right away if she just picked it up, but she still hesitated.

Why?

I love my family. They help me get through everything I need to get through. Why aren't I calling them for this?

She didn't want to speak to anyone right now. Her mind was a whirling funnel of confusion. Anger, hope, frustration, fear and so much more were intermixed in the tornado in her mind.

A list. I need to make a list. Those help me figure everything out.

Great idea. One she wasn't going to be doing for the moment because she was comfortable and had no desire to get up and move to where she kept any paper or pen. Tipping her head to the armrest, she sighed and closed her eyes.

"I don't know what you're here for, Drew. Not sure I truly want to know."

One thing she did know was how fucking good it felt to get fucked as he had done. She shuddered. God, it was heaven. Sure, she'd been sore all day. Spin class hadn't been fun in the slightest and Shai had merely watched her, but Tara swore there had been amusement in those brown eyes of hers.

Her doorbell rang and she groaned. Tightening the hold on the blanket, she put her feet into her ankle high, hot pink fuzzy slippers with the rubber sole and pink pom-poms dangling from the top and made her way to the door.

"You have a key, Shai, why didn't you just let yourself in instead of making me get up and come—"

It wasn't Shai who stood there.

Andrew leaned against the doorway, arm propped up above her head, drawing the long-sleeved shirt taut against his broad chest. Her mouth went dry and her panties got damp.

"Believe I've done that already, but trust me, baby, I'm more than ready to help you do so again."

"What are you doing here? Better question, how did you find out where I lived?"

He dragged his fingers down the side of her face and she wanted to kick herself for the way she leaned into his touch. Before she knew what had happened, they were back inside her place, the door shut and his amazing mouth on hers.

Tara sank into him, wrapping her fingers in his shirt, anchoring him as close as she could to her. When he pulled back, her mind had stopped and all she could think about was him pushing his long, thick cock inside her needy pussy.

With another gentle touch along her face, he then carried her to the sofa and set her down before joining her.

"Hi," he murmured, brushing some strands of hair from her face.

"Drew, answer my question."

I have got to keep my wits about me. This man is dangerous to me.

"Wendy told me."

Well, that did it. That one phrase yanked her from the idyllic cocoon his touch and kiss had encircled her and dropped her head first into frigid arctic waters.

"Of course she did." Her tone as warm as the North Pole.

He shook his head, eyes narrowing. "Do *not* start that again."

She curled up tighter and increased her grip on the blanket around her. "Get out."

"Fuck that." He yanked her close to him, in fact, she lay sprawled over him. "There is nothing between her and me."

"Yet, whenever we're together, her name comes up. I'm surprised that you didn't call her name out in bed last night."

"She wants to meet you, you know." He sprawled his hand along the small of her back, singeing her even though the blanket was between his skin and hers, as was her pajama top.

"I don't give a damn what your whore wants. Let me go and get out. In fact, why don't you just go back to Switzerland or wherever you're living now."

"I'm not leaving without you."

"So you're moving to America then?"

He sighed. And fuck him, even that was sexy. Made her want to nuzzle him under the chin and allow that rasp of his facial hair to do more of the abrading it had done between her legs, along her breasts and more.

"Tara."

She smacked at him and shoved away, scrambling to the other end of the couch. Pissed he had her comfort blanket, she glowered at him across the darkened room. Her glare didn't do much when he couldn't see her.

"Turn on a light, Tara, or I'll find something else to do in the dark."

Seconds later, a soft glow filled the space they were in. He scowled in her direction, frustration lining his face. For a moment, she wanted to reach out and smooth it away.

"What? There is not any point to this. We shouldn't even have gotten married in the first place. It wasn't love, it was nothing more than lust. I'll have the papers drawn up tomorrow."

"No. I don't want to divorce you. I want you to come home."

She rolled her eyes and looked around her place. Not much of a home like Shai's was. Truth was, she didn't want to be here. She had loved Switzerland and loved traveling. There weren't many objects aside from family pictures up in her apartment.

Exhaling once, sharp, she sat ramrod straight and crossed her legs. "Okay, explain it to me. Why?"

He furrowed his brow. "Why what?"

"Why, after all this time, do you suddenly *need* me to come home?"

"I said *want*. We're married and I was arrogant enough to think you would eventually come back and be there where you didn't have to do anything except what you wanted."

She scoffed and shook her head.

"Listen to me, Tara. I know you think I didn't listen to you. That somehow, once we were in Switzerland, I was different and only cared about myself. That's not true."

"Bullshit." Restless, she wrapped her fingers around the mug, grateful for the residual heat.

A muscle flexed in his jaw. "Okay, tell me why you feel so strongly about this."

"It's not my job to tell you anything."

"Fucking Christ, Tara. I want to work this out but I can't figure out how to fix this if you won't talk to me." He shoved a large hand through his hair.

Drew was large all over, even more so when compared to her.

"I told you this, Drew. You changed when we disembarked in Switzerland. You were different."

"I wasn't. My feelings toward you hadn't changed either."

"Again, I'm calling bullshit. You didn't laugh, you barely smiled and you only showed me any affection behind closed doors. You took great pleasure in ordering me around and informing me what I could or would be doing once I moved there. You made all these goddamn decisions without talking to me first. You never once *asked* me if I wanted to live there."

He opened his mouth then closed it, and she could see the wheels turning in his head. She didn't speak, waited for him to figure this out.

"Okay, I'll give you that I was a bit more serious. But I was just getting my work off the ground and had to focus on that."

"If that's where you needed to focus, perhaps you shouldn't have gotten married to someone who may have competed for any attention."

"Don't start that, Tara."

"You just admitted you had other places to focus, I'm not *starting* anything." She hopped to her feet and went to the kitchen. This was going to require having something to chew on or she was going to lose her shit.

Andrew stared at her ass in the pink flannel pants as she stomped to the kitchen. A smile tugged up his lips even as he rose to follow her. It was hard to take her seriously when she looked like a tiny pink pixie. And yet, he knew better than most she *was* serious.

"Maybe that wasn't the right way to put it."

"Hope you're better with your deals and your verbiage than you are here with me."

He leaned in the kitchen's doorway and watched her fix a cracker and cheese plate. Compared to Shai's kitchen, this one had less personality. It was all shiny and spotless, but he knew she didn't do a lot of cooking there.

He went to her fridge and pulled out some fruit then washed it in the sink. Searching through some drawers, he found a knife and cut up a portion of it.

"I listened to you in Thailand, Tara. More than you will ever know."

Aliyah Burke

"Prove it." She popped a piece of white cheddar in her mouth.

Placing the last of the red grapes in a bowl, he nodded. "Very well." Andrew moved around the island and got behind her, nuzzling her along the shell of her ear. "You talked about your dream."

"I'm living it."

"No, Tara, you're not. You want to be a lawyer for the ICC."

She stilled beneath him and he pressed closer, loving the feel of her against him.

"You want to have an office in the Hauge and prosecute some of their cases. Being an ADA isn't anything to scoff at by any means, but that's not what you ultimately want."

"I mentioned that one night after we'd been drinking."

"I listened. I do listen to you, Tara. I know you think that when we got home, I changed. I suppose in a way I did, but I didn't mean to hurt you by it. And when you left, I was arrogant in my assumption you would come back. I was thinking that you would be swayed by what I had and could offer you."

"I never wanted money from you. I didn't know you were a baron until after you married me."

"I know." He moved her hair to the side, grateful it was loose around her shoulders—he loved the thick, silken waves. Pressing a line of kisses to the graceful curve of her neck, he smiled as she moaned and angled her head to give him better access.

"I don't want any woman other than you, Tara. I don't know how to get you to realize this. I want you at my side. I want my ring back on your finger, and I want you to use your proper last name."

"Why does it matter what name I use?"

"Because I want the world to know that of all the millions of choices you had to pick as a man, you picked me."

She shook her head and reached for another piece of cheese. "That's not even logical."

"Why not?" He captured her wrist and brought her hand with the cheese to his mouth, allowing his lips to loiter over her fingers as he took the food from her. Swallowing, he fed her one. "I'm proud of my wife."

"I don't know anymore, Drew. Words are just words."

"True." The statement had the potential to gut him— however, he held on to some hope because she didn't state a flat-out no. It was an opening, a chance. He had no intention of letting this one slip by. "So give me a chance to prove it."

"And how do you plan on doing that?"

"Give me some time to be here and be your husband. Let me meet your family, well, the rest of them." She didn't relax—in fact, she grew tenser. "Or, we could go somewhere and relearn one another."

Tara ducked under his arm and headed back to the couch, the plate of food in one hand. He followed with the fruit. Despite her setting her dish in the middle of the coffee table so it could be reached from both sides, he didn't sit across from her, instead reclaiming a seat beside her on the couch.

She angled herself so her back was to the arm, crossed her legs, and watched him. Her black eyes sharp and assessing. He held still. He understood she had to process what he was offering. Her life would be different once it came out that she was not only married, but had been for five years. He got that, but didn't care. He wanted the world to know.

"May I ask you something?" He fixed himself a buttery cracker with a cube of cheddar. He chewed it while she worked her lower lip.

"Go ahead."

"We— What happened when you got shot and why didn't you contact me when that happened?"

"It was a disgruntled defendant." She shrugged. "Happens. And I didn't see the point in reaching out to you. Honestly, I didn't know if I could get in touch with you, wasn't sure if your number was the same."

The words she didn't say...that she didn't even thought about reaching out or contacting him—that burned more than anything he'd ever care to admit.

"It's the same. I won't change it." His palms burned to draw her close to him. "Are you okay?"

He'd seen the scar last night as he'd kissed every inch of her body. It had filled him with fury, even now— thinking about it did not do a damn thing to calm him down.

"I'm fine." A grin lifted her lips. "You'd think getting a bullet dug out of me would have entitled me to a bit of a break from Shai, but no, it didn't. Bitch still makes me go to spin class with her."

"Spin class?"

"Yes, you know the class you pay good money where some sadist ass sits in front of you and yells while you pedal and sweat?"

His laughter slid free. "But damn, you have one hell of an ass."

Her smile was full of seduction and pleasure. "Thank you. It's important, you know, to make sure of that."

Warning bells rang and he shook his head. Reaching out to cup her chin, he leaned close and kissed her once. "I think it's about the time you get to spend with your sister, therefore, it's worth all the pain and sweat."

"Maybe." Her eyes sparkled setting off the tone of her response.

"So what happened to him?"

She busied herself with fixing some more crackers and looked up at him through a sheet of her hair. "Who?"

"The man who shot you."

"Oh, him."

Andrew was baffled by the way she talked about being shot, almost like it hadn't mattered she'd nearly had her life snuffed out.

Like she would be in less danger working and prosecuting for the ICC.

He swallowed and forced himself to a calm state. Eating some grapes, he waited for her to respond.

"He was put in jail."

Andrew watched her expression, hoping to see some flicker of something. Anything, really, that would show she had been bothered by the action. Again, he was disappointed.

"You should have called me."

She shrugged. He reached between them and gripped her wrist. She tipped her head up and watched him.

"Do you have *any* idea how fucking worried I was when Wendy told me you'd been shot?" Her eyes narrowed but he kept going. "Of course not. And why is that? Because you couldn't be *bothered* to speak to me. Couldn't be hassled to reach out to let *your husband* know you'd been shot."

So much for keeping calm about this.

"I'm surprised your precious Wendy didn't tell you I was fine. Or hell, perhaps she was waiting to tell you that I'd died so you two could be together, all legal like."

Andrew matched her glare for glare. His own temper spiked and he was spoiling for a fight.

"How many times do I have to tell you that there's nothing, not a goddamn thing, between myself and Wendy? She's my personal assistant, that's it. Nothing more, nothing less."

"Maybe I just don't believe you."

Stuffing his desire to shake her, he fisted his hands and kept him in his lap. His father may have been an abusive bastard but he would never raise his hand to a woman.

"Regardless of that fact, Tara, I'm still your husband and I deserve to know when something like that happens."

She reached up with her left hand and tucked some hair behind her ear as she watched him, her gaze sharp and assessing. "So you're saying, because we're married, a couple, that large decisions should be shared. Or large events should be shared between us. Is that what I'm hearing you say? Is that your whole reason for being upset that I never reached out when I got shot?"

Trap. Trap. Trap.

Ignoring his subconscious, Andrew nodded. "Exactly." He was thrilled she was seeing it and understanding it from his point of view because, to be honest, it was getting very frustrating having to repeat himself and struggling to make her understand where he was coming from.

She pursed her lips briefly, nodded, then leaned back against the couch. With the fingers of her right hand, she trailed them along her knee as she went over some thoughts within her mind. Then she lifted her gaze and held his.

"If that's the case, why didn't you tell me about your business holdings in this big merger plan that you have going on that Wendy needed you to read over all these papers and send back to her for?"

Andrew opened his mouth, not positive how she'd found out about all this, only to snap it shut when she slashed her hand through the air.

"It was a rhetorical question, Drew. I really don't care to know your excuse. You're upset about the other thing for no other reason than because you think you have a right to everything that goes on in my life, but have a right as the man to keep whatever you're doing to yourself." She pushed to her feet and glared down at him from her unimpressive height. "I'm done. Don't come back into my life toting holier-than-thou crap when you're doing the exact same thing I was. You have no right to be pissed at me any more than I have a right to be pissed at you."

Andrew lifted his hand once more and she shook her head.

"I'm not finished. We're both adults and I can take full responsibility for my actions. Maybe you should do the same with yours before you try to come and make it seem like I'm the one who fucked up this marriage. Show yourself out. Good night, Drew. And goodbye."

Within seconds he was left alone in her living room as the storm outside got worse. Tipping his head forward, Andrew pinched the bridge of his nose and swore in multiple languages. Tara was right. Again. He had handled this entire thing incorrectly and all he'd managed was to push her farther away from him, which was the last thing he'd wanted. He wanted her back. He wanted her in his life. He wanted to keep his wife.

Stretching out his legs, he hooked his hands behind his head and thought about his options at that point in time. His gaze drifted down the hall where she had disappeared and a smile tugged up his lips.

"I don't think it's going to be that easy, baby. Not this time."

Chapter Seven

She stirred and froze when the strong arm around her midsection tightened, anchoring her back into him. Tara's mind raced with all the possibilities of what could've happened last night that would have this end result of her lying in bed with a man.

All I did was confront Drew, have wild crazy sex with him, go to my sister's then come back here and tell him to leave. I didn't go out drinking after. So there shouldn't be a man in my bed.

Not that any of that mattered. Tara knew without a doubt who was lying in this bed with her. The one man she could never forget no matter how hard she tried. The man she'd married. And the one she'd told last night to leave her apartment. Also known as the man who had not listened to her and had climbed into bed with her as if he belonged there.

Opening her eyes just enough to see the digital readout on her clock, Tara allowed them to drift back shut when she saw the time. Three in the morning.

Early even for her to be getting up after the night she'd had last night. Besides, what was the harm in indulging herself one last time with what was like to lie in his strong embrace?

After all, he was here, as she was. Obviously, he wasn't going to go anywhere, because he hadn't left when she'd told him to leave the first time. She flicked her tongue over her lips and settled down, allowing his heat at her back combined with the blankets over them both to escort her once more into a land of slumber.

She woke an hour later when her Fitbit buzzed its silent alarm. She did not want to get up, especially knowing what awaited her the moment she crawled out from under the blankets. Her sister and that sadistic bitch of a spin class instructor.

Indulging for another two minutes before she forced herself out of bed, Tara rubbed her eyes as she made her way to the kitchen to start her coffee. What she wanted was a hot shower to work out her sore muscles, but it was pointless to take a shower before spin class. Lord knew she never left there any less than completely drenched with sweat.

Once her coffee percolated, she returned to her bedroom and turned on the lights, all without care for the man who still lay in her bed.

Drew groaned and opened his eyes, pinning her to the spot. "That's not nice, darling."

"I have to go to spin class, so you need to get up and leave. I'll drop you off at your hotel on my way."

He stretched with a languid motion, drawing all her attention to the rippled pectorals and defined abdomen before her gaze trailed down to the tented sheet. Her mouth dried out and she tried to focus on something other than the happy trail she longed to follow with her tongue.

"With or without clothes, Drew. It's your choice, I don't care."

If he was perturbed by her comments or her surly morning attitude, he never once let it show. Instead he sat up, swung his legs over and rose before she could even prepare herself for the sight of him completely naked and one hundred percent hard. The whimper slid free and she had no time to attempt to contain it.

His cock rose long and thick from the dark thatch of pubic hair. Her gaze riveted to it, watching it move as he approached. The broad head, swollen and angry, had a few pearls of pre-cum, making it glisten. Every urge within her begged her to drop to the floor and take him in her mouth. Tara locked her knees to keep from doing that very thing.

"You know my choice, Tara. With you it's always been sans clothing. I look at you and I want nothing more than to sink my cock into your hot pussy. Or lift you until you wrap your legs around my head and neck, giving me unfettered access to lick and eat that sweet pussy. I want you tight around my head, hands ripping at my hair as I make you come over and over again."

It took her two tries to get the words together to force them past her lips. And when she did, they were less than impressive, more like a wheeze or a prayer instead of a strong, assertive statement.

"I'm leaving in ten minutes."

Tara marched past him, determined not to look at him or his fantastic body a moment longer. She went into her closet and pulled out some spin class gear. When she stepped back out he was gone — however, she heard the bathroom fan running. Taking advantage of the opportunity while she had it, she shoved into her clothes and made sure to be out in the kitchen by the time he joined her.

His eyes still smoldered, just as they always had when he watched her with passion in them. She hated it. Hated that he could still make her revisit all those moments they'd shared during their week together in the brief time before she realized his life wasn't hers.

"What are you thinking about?"

She continued fixing her coffee how she liked it, keeping her gaze on the mug in front of her. "Just thinking of things and how they used to be. Realizing how much we both changed and how different our lives are."

He maneuvered over so he was by her shoulder. With a slight tug of her hair, which was up in a ponytail, he held her head back until he leaned down and brushed her lips together in a gentle yet altogether branding kiss.

"Our lives don't have to be on different paths, Tara. In fact, I'd much prefer they were on the same path, or at least heading to the same destination."

"You have businesses to run and I have a job to do. My work is here, yours isn't. I don't see how we will ever be on the same path or going in the same direction." She snapped the lid on her travel mug and ignored the spike of pain piercing her heart.

"So that's it then? We see each other, fuck and go on about our lives as if this time together never happened?"

"I don't know what more you want from me. I can't do my job from Switzerland. And I highly doubt you and Wendy are moving over here."

There'd been a hardness in his eyes when she'd first started. However, by the time she finished her statement, his gaze had changed to soft and, dare she say, caring.

"That sounded like a challenge, Tara Coleman." He kissed her again then stepped back and walked to the door where he waited for her, coat in hand.

No words were exchanged between them as they went down to her car. As usual, he held the door for her, closing it behind her before he got in on the passenger side. He remained silent for the ride back to his hotel. As she idled before the entrance he unhooked his belt and leaned over, dragging a knuckle down the left side of her cheek, bringing her head around to face him.

"I'm not going away, Tara. Please have dinner with me tonight. No fighting, no talk about moving, no talk about Wendy. Just us, you and me."

Her heart rate tripled before it slowed. Every bit of advice she'd ever given herself told her to run. Run far, run fast, run hard and never ever look back. She opened her mouth to deliver the letdown and said, "Yes."

What the fuck just happened? I was supposed to say no. How the hell did 'yes' slip past my mouth? And why is he looking so damn smug?

"Perfect. I'll make a reservation with the restaurant for around eight. You have my number, use it if the time doesn't work, otherwise around seven." He brushed his lips over hers once more and was gone before she could even catch her breath.

Her entire way to spin class she tried to figure out how that had happened. And failed. Her breathing still hadn't returned to normal as she met up with Shai and headed inside to the torture room.

"You look like you slept well. Lots of mind-numbing sex before bed?"

Flipping her sister off, she didn't dignify that with any further answer. Fighting with Shai, or arguing as the case may be, would only result in her being even more out of breath. She didn't need to lose any more face in spin class.

Shai, bless her heart, let it go. At least verbally. There were plenty of sideways glances and condescending smirks and she struggled to keep up in the class from hell.

After they finished, she and Shai walked out to their cars and Tara searched for a way to broach the fact she couldn't have dinner with her sister tonight.

"So I have to cancel our dinner plans tonight," Shai said. "I'm starting a new cooking class and they told me the first one was tonight instead of tomorrow as it had been listed when I signed up. I'm sorry. We could do lunch, or breakfast before work if that would work better or just a rain check and wait until Eva comes back from Florida?"

"A cooking class? What the hell do you need to learn about cooking?"

Her sister shrugged, a happy smile on the face that was far too serious most of the time. "It's a course in Middle Eastern cooking and I couldn't turn down the opportunity to increase my knowledge on food from their countries." She touched Tara's shoulder, halting her forward motion. "You're okay with this, right?"

"Absolutely. I think it's great you're taking a cooking class. So long as I get to be the test subject when you have to try new dishes at home."

Shai laughed and drew her in close for a hug. "You have my promise on that."

Returning the embrace, Tara tugged on one of her sister's ear flaps. "We'll have a big get-together when Eva comes back. We have to catch up on everything Grant related."

"That's not all. We have to catch her up on you being a baroness."

"I suppose so. Let me run catch a shower and head off to work. I'll call you later in the week to see how you're doing. Love you. Bye."

She hopped into her Rogue as Shai climbed into her Subaru Outback with a wave. Moments later, each sister headed in different directions to begin their workdays.

* * * *

Andrew counted down the time until he could go pick up Tara for their date. All day, when his phone rang, he immediately got concerned that she'd found some reason to cancel or come up with some way to get out of spending any more time with him. It never came, and as the time neared for him to head to the car to pick her up, more hope had sprung into his chest. Perhaps they had a chance after all.

Before walking out of his hotel room he paused in front of the mirror and took a final look over his attire. Satisfied with what he saw, he shrugged into his full-length leather jacket, tugged on his gloves and exited the room.

As requested, his car was just outside the front door to the hotel, the driver waiting, and he opened the door right away. With a brief 'thank you', Andrew slid in over the seat. The man already knew where to go so he didn't engage in small talk—he just leaned back and focused on remaining calm instead of feeling as giddy as he had the first time she had accepted his date request.

They bypassed the plows that worked hard to keep the lanes clear as the man traversed through the city streets on his way to Tara's apartment. Once there, the driver again held the door for him as he slid free and strode to the front door. The doorman let him in with a smile and a nod.

Andrew strode over the spotless tile floor of the lobby to the elevator bay. The man at the concierge desk looked at him but didn't say a word. Once inside, he pressed the button for Tara's floor. His strides were no longer as sure as he went down the hall to her door.

With a gloved hand he rapped sharply and waited for her to answer. It took a few moments, but he heard the lock disengage prior to the door swinging open, then he lost his breath.

"Holy shit, you're beautiful."

His short-circuiting brain struggled to keep up, but it was a failed mission from the jump. He didn't understand how she did it. There wasn't any way one woman should have the ability to rob him so completely and utterly of all the breath in his body. But this woman found a way.

"Thank you."

Her hair had been gathered up in some sophisticated knot on top of her head that hid some but not all of the pink. He didn't know much in the way of evening gown information, so he couldn't tell the style. Definitely couldn't tell the designer. All he knew was how fucking hot his wife looked in the dress. Pink satin with the V-neckline and near nonexistent straps that were twisted, showing off all of her smooth olive skin.

All he wanted to do was push her back inside her apartment and rip it from her body, showing her the full extent of what the dress did to him.

He cleared his throat. "Coat?"

"On the hook." She didn't look at him but was messing with something inside the clutch that matched what she wore.

He moved past her and grabbed the wool coat. As he came up behind her to assist her with putting it on, his mouth grew drier than the Sahara. *Is she even wearing any fucking panties with that dress?* And if he asked, and she said no, was he really going to be in a better state of mind?

He brushed his lips along the bare skin of her shoulder prior to dropping the material there. Then he offered his arm and waited for her to take it to escort her to the elevator.

The ride down was silent and he still hadn't quite found his tongue as they walked arm in arm across the lobby to the door. He noticed a good number of people staring, and if it bothered her she didn't say a word. Tara kept her gaze straight ahead.

Once they were in the car heading toward the dinner spot, he picked up her hand and threaded their fingers together. That got her attention. Tara lifted her head and looked at him.

Andrew cocked an eyebrow but didn't speak. He didn't want to. Right now, them speaking led to fighting. And he wanted a nice evening with his wife.

"How was your day?"

Her question threw him almost for a moment. He was pleased she didn't try to remove her hand from his touch.

"Busy. But the hostile takeover was stopped so I'll take everything as a win."

A cute furrow appeared between her brow. "You mentioned a hostile takeover. From people within your company or those just trying to take over?"

He stretched out his legs and hooked his ankles. "A little bit of both. Mostly from the outside, but there was an inside man who was feeding them information to help them with their cause."

She snorted. "Their cause? Please tell me you don't feel sorry for them."

"I'm not that nice of a guy. I don't feel sorry for them, but they did have their own cause."

"Laziness is not a cause, Drew."

"Why do you think it was laziness?"

"The words hostile takeover. That means they want what you have, yet aren't willing to work for it. Also known as stealing. People steal because they're lazy and they don't want to put in the work with the time and effort to get what you have gotten."

He pivoted so he faced her completely. Bracing one arm on the back of the seat, he held her gaze as he stared into her eyes.

"That makes sense. But I fight for what's mine. I *won't* let it go or give it up."

Her mouth formed a tiny little 'O' before she smoothed out her expression. "I'm sure your employees are grateful."

"Possibly. I think it's more that I'm selfish and I like to keep what's mine."

She didn't back away. If anything, she inched closer. "So it's all about possessions then. Is that what I'm hearing?"

Andrew took a finger and dragged it along the edge of her dress from one shoulder, over her breast, down to the bottom of the vee and back up the other side.

Her breathing hitched. It was only by the grace of God his didn't do the same. He ran his finger along her jaw, touching her lips ever so lightly so as not to smear the gloss back up to the one wave of hair that curled down over her ear.

"I don't know what you're hearing. I'm stating clearly I won't let go of what's mine."

Her pupils dilated and that cute small nose of hers flared. Fuck, he wanted to kiss her. Last night had been a blend of heaven and hell for him. Heaven had come in the guise of being able to hold her, sleep wrapped around her, yet hell, because she was so near and yet there was a chasm between them.

The car slowed to a halt before the restaurant entrance. He bit back a curse, wanting to prolong this — whatever it was — between them. As the driver opened the door, he got out and turned back to offer his hand to Tara.

She took it, allowing him to assist her from the town car. Tara moved with ease beside him. Warmth met them as they entered and he paused by the coat check. He took a moment and gazed around the area before he reached for Tara's coat and helped her off with it. Allowing his fingers to graze along the silken smoothness of her skin, he pressed a gentle kiss at the base of her neck.

After checking her coat, he shrugged out of and removed his before handing it over. Offering his arm to her once more, he waited until she accepted before they progressed on. As he walked through toward their table, he noticed all the stares leveled in their direction by the patrons.

He couldn't be sure if it was because they were together, the way she was dressed, or whatever. Quite honestly, he didn't care—all he knew was the most beautiful woman in the room was on his arm, nobody else's. Not only that, she was his wife. After another kiss to her shoulder as he seated her, he walked around and took his own seat.

"Ready to eat something?"

Tara gave him a slight smile before she nodded.

Andrew returned it then focused on the wine list. He was going to do whatever it took to make tonight special.

Chapter Eight

Tara stood in her office, staring through the double-pane glass to the thick flakes that fell. Her mind wasn't on her task today. All she could think about was last night's dinner and the time she was able to spend with Drew.

She hadn't thought they'd be able to make it through the entire meal without some sort of argument or disagreement sprouting up. She had been wrong. Their time together had been enjoyable, fun and reminiscent of when they'd been in Thailand.

Figures, just when I'm getting over him he comes back into my life and makes it harder for me to forget.

The fact that he hadn't pushed her into letting him back up to her apartment had her thinking. Just what game was he playing? Was he on the up and up about actually wanting this to work?

She exhaled and turned away from the view, focusing instead on the massive amount of papers loitering on her desktop. *I have work to do. I can't be spinning my time dwelling over what may or may not have happened with him last night.*

Her phone rang. She snatched it from the cradle and put it up to her ear. "Monroe."

"Ms. Monroe, you've a detective out here to see you. A Detective Savvas."

With her thumb she rubbed the furl between her eyebrows as she raced to put a face to the name. Or at least the name to a case.

It hit her—he was one of the detectives who had shown up when she'd been shot.

"Send him on in, thank you."

Moments later, two sharp raps came at her door, followed by a tall, handsome detective stepping through. For a moment, she forgot she was a married woman. She skimmed him twice, taking in the brown hair, green eyes, and scruff lining his jaw.

I really don't remember him by my bed and I don't think this is a man I would forget.

"How can I help you today, Detective? Please come in and sit down."

As he turned his head and observed everything in the room, she saw the small queue that his hair been pulled back into. *And he gets hotter and hotter.*

"Thank you for seeing me, Ms. Monroe. I won't take up a lot of your time, but something's come to our attention that we felt we should bring to you."

Uncertain, she perched on the edge of her chair and noticed he didn't sit or even attempt to until after she had. Even though he reclined in the chair, she had the faintest impression that he was more like a predator lying in wait. All coiled and ready to spring into action at a moment's notice.

"And what's that?"

"We overheard some chatter from some of the inmates where your shooter is incarcerated. It appears he's put out a hit on you."

Tara exhaled and pursed her as lips she reached for a pencil and spun it in her fingers. After a few blinks, she stilled the pencil and stared at the man across from her.

"I'm not really sure how I'm supposed to react to that news. I mean, I know there are people out to get me for what I do, for who I put away and the like. However, I don't think I've ever had a direct hit put out on me before. What's the procedure? And is this threat credible or is it just an inmate talking a lot of smack to try to make bones?"

He scratched his jaw before lacing his fingers and thumping his thumbs together. "I'm inclined to believe this is a credible threat. Even if I was one hundred percent sure I would stop to err on the side of caution when it comes to an assistant district attorney. Don't get me wrong, I would be concerned were it an everyday citizen, however as it is towards you, I feel there is a bit more credibility behind it."

"Because it's me? Why, Detective, we don't know each other that well and here you are saying that you believe people would have it out for me? Did I say something to you in the hospital room after I got shot the first time for you to feel this way?"

He flashed a grin she had no doubt would drop many a pair of panties. "I like your sense of humor. I think you're going to need it. And no, you did not say anything out of line to me. I'm going to be honest, your sister, on the other hand, has read me the riot act numerous times."

Tara nodded. "Shai would be the one who would have done that. She's slightly volatile. But she means well."

"I could tell. Entire family is close, and that's one of the reasons I want you to take this so seriously. My gut is telling me if they can't get to you, they will try to go after one of your sisters or your parents."

And just like that, this wasn't as amusing anymore. Tara leaned forward, resting her arms on the desk, and held his sharp gaze. "I'll worry about me later, because I have no doubt I will have some kind of protection detail. My question is what happens with my family? Will they be protected?"

"You know as well as I do it's gonna be hard to get protection for your entire family."

She did know that. Hated it. Always had when it came to other people's families, but this was hers and it pissed her off. Royally.

"Okay, and here it is. I want my parents protected first. Then my sisters and then me. I spend most of my days here anyway. I will be protected in this building. But Eva works at the hospital and Shai is a professor at the university. Both places that are accessible for anybody wishing to do them harm."

The sergeant detective stared at her for a good minute before he nodded in a slow manner. "I'll take this up with my lieutenant and let you know what he says."

"I'm not budging on this. I knew the risks I signed on to be ADA. I knew this could happen at some point in my life. I didn't sign on and risk their lives. Make it happen. I'll also make it known that you came in and did your job but I'm fighting you every step of the way until my family has protection."

"You're the boss."

She flashed a grin. "Glad you see it my way."

He got up from his chair, gave her a sharp nod, spun on his heel and strode out without a look back. The moment the door closed behind him she buried her face in her hands and tried to control her breathing.

I have to tell my parents. And my sisters.

The question was who to tell first. Logically she should let Shai know, get her on board with the entire situation and then go to her parents with backup. When she pulled out her phone to send her sister a text, she got a call from her boss.

That would have to be addressed later. She hurried out of the office and into his to see what it was he needed. The rest of the day passed by in a blur of paperwork and impending migraine. She was late leaving again and had just waved to Marcus when she looked outside the door to see Drew waiting there on the front steps.

There was no stopping the smile that tipped up the corners of her mouth as she neared him. Pushing into the cold, she peered up at him and cocked an eyebrow.

"What exactly are you doing here, Drew?"

"What else would I be doing here? I came to see my wife."

"You saw me last night at dinner."

"And I'm hoping to see you tonight at dinner as well."

She rolled her lower lip in her teeth and made a moment's decision. "Give me a minute."

She dug in her pocket and pulled out her cell phone. After a quick text to her parents and her sister, she moved closer to the man she'd married, soaking up the warmth he exuded as they stood there in the falling snow.

Tara waited for the response, then she took his arm and headed for her car. "Dinner is fine. But it's not just going to be me. You can meet the rest of the family aside from Eva, who's not here."

Drew halted, in effect stopping her as well, then he looked down at her. "Why the change of heart? Not that I'm not grateful, but I'm a bit suspicious considering you wanted to keep me hidden from everybody."

"I'm not giving any reasons until we get to dinner. You can come or not, it's up to you, but the offer is there."

"Oh you can bet your ass I'm going. I'm just curious as to why."

"I guess you'll find out at dinner. We should get going."

She didn't say anything on the way over to her parents' house. Instead she took the time to figure out the best way to broach this. There wasn't going to be a chance to get Shai on her side ahead of time, and to top it all off, now she would have a husband who no doubt would have an opinion on how this needed to play out.

Her nervousness had ratcheted up to well past ten by the time she pulled into their driveway. Christmas decorations were still up and her mother wouldn't take them down until the new year, it was just how she was. She parked beside her sister's Outback. In the time it took her to gather her breath, Drew had gotten out and was around to her side of the car to open it.

As they approached the door she noticed he was carrying something in his arm.

"What do you have there?"

"A bottle of wine I was going to give to you. Your parents drink wine, don't they? Or should I say our parents?"

Her response was stifled because the front door opened and she found herself staring at her mother. She looked so much like Eva it never failed to make her smile. Within seconds, Tara was engulfed by a powerful hug.

"Look at me getting all mushy out here in the cold. Forgive me. Come in, come on in out of the cold and where it's warm."

Shai and her father were inside and both turned to observe them as they stepped into the foyer. No flicker of recognition moved over her sister's face, and Tara wasn't sure what to make of that.

"I know tonight wasn't our typical family night for a meal, so thank you for allowing us to do this. I have some news to share with everyone and some news to share with Mom and Dad." She wished her hair was looser so she could shove her fingers through it. "I got a visit today from one of the detectives who was there when I got shot and he told me that there is a hit out on me."

Her parents and Drew all gasped and began talking. Shai remained silent and cocked an eyebrow. Holding out her hands, Tara implored them to pipe down. When silence once again reigned, she took another breath and looked at everyone in the room.

"We're working on establishing protection for everyone and no, it's nonnegotiable." Ignoring her mother's open mouth, because she knew what was coming, Tara continued. "The reason the gentleman beside me is here is for one reason only. His name is Andrew Coleman, Baron Andrew Coleman, and he's my husband."

She angled her head and looked up at Drew. "Now you know."

She'd just thrown him to the sharks. Or was it wolves? Perhaps it was just quicksand. Either way, it wasn't at all how he'd intended to be introduced to the family. Still, he had to give her credit that she wasn't hiding it any longer. He wrapped an arm around her waist and dropped a kiss to her temple before stepping slightly in front of her as if to shelter her from the impending storm he knew was about to explode.

"Nice to meet you both." He held out the bottle of wine to her father and waited for him to accept it then he followed it up with a handshake. "Andrew Coleman."

His father-in-law watched him with sharp blue eyes. "Frederick Monroe." He set the wine down and turned to his wife. "Adalyn Monroe."

Andrew extended his hand toward her. "Ma'am, it's an honor to meet you. I've heard so much about you."

Pain filled her eyes as she watched him. "I've never heard a thing about you."

Beside him, he could feel Tara stiffen at the words her mother uttered.

"We need to hear a little bit more about this hit on our daughter, Mother. Then we will address why our middle child didn't see fit to tell her parents she had gotten married, but from the looks of things, told her baby sister, who doesn't seem all that surprised by this news. Then again, she also doesn't seem all that surprised about the hit on her either. Maybe we're just the last to know everything now."

Shai didn't defend anything, just sat there and waited. Her mother wiped her eyes and walked past them all with her head high.

"Well, I won't be one to neglect my guests. We can talk while we eat."

The others followed her into the kitchen, and Andrew stopped Tara and drew her to his chest.

"Hell of a way to spring this on me, Tara. As much as I want to be pissed at you right now for doing what you did, I think you need all the people you can have in your corner at the moment." He brushed his lips over the corner of her mouth. "I always have your back."

She squeezed his hand but didn't say a word. They went to the kitchen and moved through to the dining area, where everyone else had already taken a seat. Andrew held her chair for her, sliding her in before taking his own at her right side. To his right sat Frederick.

"What does this mean exactly, Tara?" her father asked once grace had been said.

"It means everybody gets protection. I don't know for how long the detective said they're working on it, but they do believe it's a credible threat and is not one to take lightly."

"Are you having protection assigned you as well?"

Tara looked to the other end of the table where her mother sat, pain still in her eyes. "Yes, ma'am, I am. But I refused to accept it until they could tell me everybody else was safe. Protection will be put together for Eva when she gets back. Hopefully this'll get wrapped up soon and nobody's lives will be too messed up. I'm sorry about all this."

Adalyn dropped her fork on her plate, the clatter bringing everybody's attention to her. "This? This is what you're upset about? Us having to be protected because you're doing your job very well. But you're not upset about keeping your marriage from your parents? From your sisters? At least Eva."

Again, Andrew expected Shai to step up and say she had just learned that they'd been married. She didn't. Correcting assumptions was never done, instead she took some of the brunt of the withering and pained looks from their parents. His heart went out to her a little more.

They truly do protect one another.

"How long have you been married to my daughter? Apparently I need to speak to you since she is incapable of giving me straight answers."

He set down the wine glass and focused his full attention on her mother. Correction, his mother-in-law.

"We've been married for five years." Her mouth dropped open and tears swam in those blue eyes. "This isn't all her fault, ma'am. It's mine too. We've had a rocky marriage and at times weren't sure if it was going to continue. I haven't even been in the States for these past few years and it just seemed easier for neither of us to say anything." He reached over and captured Tara's hand in his own.

"Please know this was never an intentional slight to hurt either one of you or her sisters. Tara loves you all so much and has never said anything but the most amazing things about you. I know this feels like a betrayal and I get it, but we felt it best to go this way. Especially when we couldn't always get along. We didn't want it splashed all over the news about how this young ADA for the Quad Cities was having issues with her husband who happens to be a baron. I hope you can understand that."

Tara opened her mouth so he squeezed her hand until she closed it and lowered her gaze. He had no trouble shouldering the brunt of this for her. Across the table from him, Shai met and held his gaze. When no one was looking he gave her a wink. It wasn't returned but when she lifted her glass the next time for a drink, she tipped it toward him in acknowledgment. That he would take.

Throughout the rest of the meal talk swung between the protection they would have, and what he did, and where he lived currently. The woman beside him was subdued and he didn't like it at all. This wasn't the Tara he had known and fallen for. This one reminded him of someone who'd been beaten and put down.

After the meal was over and had been cleaned up, he sat in the living room while Tara spoke to her parents. A little bit later, Shai came in and sat beside him on the couch. She didn't face the same direction he did — no, she turned to face him direct and had her feet up on the couch cross-legged.

"You and I had a talk when you were at my place and you didn't answer me when I questioned you about what your plans were for her. I figured you didn't think that you owed it to me to explain anything. And that you two should discuss it with each other before you said anything." She shrugged. "While I find that annoying, I can see your point on that. However, after your behavior tonight, I'm thinking you have every intention of staying married to my sister, which then, by default, will make you my brother-in-law."

He rested the ankle of one boot on his opposite knee. "And this is a problem?"

"Hell no." She scooted closer on the cushion until her knees almost brushed against his thigh. "However, I'm not above bribery and wanting to get what I want. I want to know if you have any pull with any of the cooking schools over there."

He wasn't all that sure where this was going. "You want to come to Switzerland to learn to cook? You already know how to cook and you are a damn good one from what I've seen."

"What I want from Switzerland is the chocolate and the cooking. What better place to go and cook? Not strictly to learn but also for the atmosphere around you. Being able to look out on the Alps…what an experience that must be."

"If that's what you want, I take my duty seriously as your older brother to get it for you."

She flashed him a grin that bespoke complete impishness. As quick as it came it was gone and he was left with the woman he'd seen throughout dinner. Quiet. Assessing. Watchful. Shai inched back so they were no longer nearly touching. She just managed to swing around and put her feet on the floor when the others came back into the room.

Tara walked over and settled on the cushion between them. Andrew draped an arm around her shoulders, tucking her tight to his side. She rested her head on his shoulder when he pulled the tie from the end of her braid and began to release her hair. Her exhaustion seeped from her and he knew it was time to get her going so she could get some rest. Even with that knowledge, it was another two hours before they finally made their departure from his in-laws.

Outside, he escorted her to the passenger side and gave a sharp shake of his head when she opened her mouth to dispute him.

"Don't."

He slid behind the wheel, started the engine and backed out of the drive.

"Do you even have a driver's license for here?"

"International driver's license. Trust me, Tara, I wouldn't do anything to hurt you."

"So you say now," she muttered. "Just wait until you have to go back to Switzerland."

Andrew flexed his fingers along the steering wheel. He wasn't about to get into this with her, not right now. Especially since he wasn't sure she'd meant for him to hear her comment.

He knew the way back to her place and had every intention of spending the night with her. Sex wouldn't be necessary, but would be a bonus, as it always was with her. He put the car in gear and headed home.

Even now, I think of anywhere with her as home.

Tara was silent as he slowed for a red light. He gazed over at her. She was out cold. Lashes resting against her cheek, she appeared at peace for the first time since he'd seen her tonight. The stress lining her eyes at her parents' house had gone.

If only I could erase the circles from her below her eyes, too.

He parked in her spot and even when he lifted her in his arms, she never made a peep.

Chapter Nine

The heavy veil of sleep lifted from Tara's eyes as she slowly came alert. Barely any light came through and what did was a muted gray.

Still snowing.

She sat up and ran her gaze over the baggy T-shirt covering her body. Nothing else. Not even a pair of panties.

What the fuck happened last night? She lay back, physically and emotionally exhausted.

I remember telling all about the hit on me, the protection they were all going to need and —

She bolted back up again, jackknifing in the bed.

I told them about Drew.

It all came rushing back. The look of betrayal from both parents, but most of all the one from her mom, Adalyn. Tears sprang up at the recollection. Fighting them back, she frowned as she stared at her bedroom door. Almost shut. She slept with it open. Always.

Is Drew here? Tara sighed. *If he is here, would it truly be so bad?*

She didn't think so. However, lying there wondering did not help her, so she decided to find out.

Later.

Later turned out to be mere moments when she heard male voices in the outer space of her apartment. Not voice, *voices.*

Spurred into action, she exited her bedroom and went to the living area, where she stopped short at the view before her. Drew stood there talking to Detective Savvas and two uniformed officers.

In fact, he acted like he owned the area. There was also the matter of his state of dress. Or the lack thereof. Dress pants were the single article on him and he didn't seem at all perturbed by that as he conversed with the men.

Pivoting on her heels, she retreated for some pants at least. It wouldn't do for her to be entertaining officers of the law in a shirt.

The men were still conversing when she returned. Drew gazed at her, a private smile tipping up his bow-shaped lips. "Morning, beautiful." He gestured to her.

She was over halfway to him before she realized he was ordering her around in her own place. Furious she'd responded to his beckon, she scowled at him.

Doesn't even give a damn. His smile never left his face and when she got beside him, he kissed her as he wrapped an arm around her waist. Her gut tightened as she pressed up against his warm body. *His hard body.*

The man smelled divine. She didn't know how he did it, not to mention if he'd been with her all night. No way she had anything in her place that would have him smelling like this. Because if she had, she'd have clothes in it so she could wear his smell even when they weren't together.

"The guys and I were just talking."

She struggled to control her eyebrow from jacking up at his statement of the 'the guys,' as in her mind they should have been there only in an official capacity, not for setting up a time to head out to the local ball park for a beer and a game.

Sliding her gaze over to the detective, she held his for a moment before saying. "Morning, Detective."

If he was uneasy by standing in her place talking to her husband—who, until a few days ago, no one had known she had—he didn't show it. If she wasn't mistaken, there was amusement lingering in his gaze.

"Ma'am," he said.

"Ms. Monroe is fine." Drew's hold on her tightened but he didn't contradict her statement. "Are we discussing the protection on my family?"

The man nodded. "Yes. I was telling your husband that we've assigned units to your parents and to your sister. As soon as we hear that your sister is back in town, we'll have another on her. As it is, we've alerted Orlando PD about the situation and they've agreed to have a unit on her while she's down there, all without letting her know she's got plainclothes on her. We figured you would want to tell her."

Stepping away from Drew, she reached out her hand to the man before her, held his green gaze and said with heartfelt thanks, "I can't thank you enough for taking this seriously in regards to my family."

He shook her hand, his grip strong and sure. "I'm glad to be of service, even though it sucks we have to. These two, Officers Kellen and Markowitz, will be around. Please don't try to lose them. Our goal here is to keep you alive, not spend time trying to hunt you down in order to do so."

Drew returned her to his side, his large body sheltering her even further. "I have no problem paying for protection on her or her family."

Savvas shifted his weight. "We're cops, Baron Coleman, not private contractors. So thank you, but we don't need it."

Drew didn't hesitate. "Does she?" He cleared his throat. "Do they? Look, Detective, I am not about to lose my wife because your police force is understaffed and stretched thin. I know you have a lot of territory to cover and if it's something that would be fine, I'll hire personal protection for the entire group of them."

She kept her mouth shut, knowing Drew well enough to know he wasn't joking. Maybe she did know him better than she'd been trying to convince herself she did.

The detective didn't hesitate either. "I can't tell you how to spend your money. We protect our own and she's part of our family. If you do decide to bring in personal protection, I would simply ask that you let us know who they are and what they look like so we don't spend time and resources trying to make sure they are men or women who are okay to have around your family."

She licked her lips and cleared her throat. "I don't think it will be necessary to bring in any personal protection."

"You're my wife," he uttered, his voice no longer friendly or easygoing.

"And I like to think we have the best cops in the country. They're damn good at their job."

"Fine, we'll do it your way, *for now*."

"I should get going. They'll be downstairs when you are ready to head to work."

Tara gave them a smile before they left. The detective remained by the door, hand on the wood. "Thank you for your cooperation."

"I know how this works, Detective. Can I ask who you have on my family?"

"Some of our best are on your family. Sergeant Torres is on your father during the day. Officer Patron is on your mother and your sister." He paused and flipped through a small notebook he'd pulled from his pocket. He gave a heavy sigh. "She's being difficult. Right now, it's Officer Meshton."

"I'll talk to her. Thank you."

His smile was a bit strained as he nodded. "Yes, ma'am. Have a good day and thank you for your time."

The door closed behind him and seconds later it was just her and Drew. She stepped away from him and scowled. "Who the fuck do you think you are to allow men into my apartment and discuss my safety while I'm sleeping?"

"Wow, an entire five seconds before you lit into me after he left." There wasn't any emotion in his tone and that bothered her. "You're still my wife, Tara, even if you are trying not to remember that fact. I'm still here because I carried you in last night, as you were exhausted and passed out before we even got here after leaving your parents. And before you ask, yes, I undressed you."

She stared into his blue gaze for a bit. Acknowledging she'd been a bitch, she thought about what to say but settled on, "Thank you."

That got him. The widening of his eyes told her that. About to head into the kitchen, she halted at his light touch on her arm. Lifting an eyebrow, she waited for him to say something.

"I'll always protect you, Tara. You have to know this. And I want you have more protection. The best money can buy."

"I trust the cops in my city to keep us safe."

His gaze shuttered. "More than me."

"That's not it, Drew."

"Andrew."

She quirked an eyebrow. "That's what you want to quibble about right now?"

He shook his head and waved a hand in her direction.

"The cops of this city know the city. Know the family that has put this hit out on me. Honestly, I think they are more than capable of keeping us safe."

"That so?"

She crossed her arms. "I just stated that, didn't I?"

"Then explain your scowls when the names were listed. Not the one on your father but the other two. Is it because they're just officers and not holding any rank? Or is it because you don't think they can do anything if something were to happen?"

She hated being caught like this. "I'm sure they'll be fine."

He crossed his arms. "Don't lie to either of us. What are you thinking?"

"Nothing," she protested.

"Tara." There was warning in his tone.

With a frustrated sigh, she marched into the kitchen, making her way to the coffee maker. She drew short on her heels. The man didn't speak — he didn't have to. She felt him around her. Always had. *Always will. At least until he is no longer part of my life.*

He blocked her in with his strong arms. *Shit, he still hasn't put on a shirt.* It wasn't fair to tempt her with all of this muscled fineness.

"I'm not moving until you tell me. And personally, I hope you take a long time, because then I get to be pressed up to you like this. Gives me time to get you thinking about something else."

"Shai," she squeaked as his hard erection brushed against her ass. "She's going to be a problem. She hates having someone shadow her. Unless it pertains to her school schedule. This Officer Meshton is going to have her work cut out for her."

He nibbled along the skin of her bare shoulder. She shivered and cursed her weakness, even as she tipped her head more to give him more access to her needy skin.

"So, talk to her. Make your point of how much you need her to go along with this. If not for her, but for your own state of mind. I see how she protects you, even though she holds the title of the youngest."

"How do you know this?"

"I saw this last night. She could have corrected what your parents assumed happened and the length of time she'd known about me, but she didn't. She shouldered some of the blame and angry stares. She'd move mountains for you if you needed it." He shifted his hand up beneath her shirt, skimming his calloused palm along her belly, and she trembled.

"Okay," she admitted on a sigh. "I'll talk to her later today."

"Damn," he whispered against her ear. "I was hoping I would get to change your mind."

She turned in his embrace. "You did."

* * * *

"Dammit, Wendy, this is starting to piss me off."

"I'm so sorry *my* handling of *your* things isn't to your liking. Perhaps you should drag your wife back and handle it yourself."

Frowning over the actual anger in her tone, he pulled up short from the pacing he'd begun in front of Tara's large picture window that showed off a stunning landscape of the Quad Cities area.

"Wendy?"

"What?" she growled. "If all you're going to do is snap at me, then I'm done. I am following *your* instructions to the letter, so don't get mad at me because it's not going how you wanted it to."

"Fuck the deal, Wendy. What's going on with you? I've never heard you like this before. What's the problem? Who do I have to kill?"

She hesitated and that again threw him, for this woman didn't hesitate. Wendy was a woman of action, even if she wasn't one hundred percent confident in what she was about to do. She still went in without the slightest bit of hesitation. So for him to hear hesitation in her tone was more than a tiny bit disturbing.

"I don't need you to kill anyone on my behalf, Mr. Coleman."

He narrowed his eyes at his reflection in the window. Behind him, he watched the front door, waiting for Tara to come home from her day of work.

"What's with the Mr. Coleman? Christ, Wendy, if you need me to come back, tell me and I'll be on the first plane. I'm not concerned about the deal, I mean, yes, it will suck royally if I lose this deal, but if keeping the deal means I lose you, then it's not worth it to me. You're more important."

"I don't need you to come back, Mr. Coleman. It will be handled, as you pay me to do so."

"Don't you hang up this phone."

"Ms. Grider, I'm going to need you to put the phone down so we can run some more tests."

"What the fuck is going on?"

His demand went unanswered as the phone clicked off. With a low growl, he redialed her number and swore another litany of curses when it was directed straight to her voicemail.

"What's wrong?"

He snapped his gaze up to the glass and met Tara's reflection in the smooth surface.

"Something with Wendy. She was with a doctor and she's never sick."

"Then what are you doing here?"

Her question startled him. He wasn't sure exactly what she meant by that, nor was it what he'd been expecting her to say.

"What do you mean?"

She blinked and held his gaze with unerring calmness. Red flags popped up.

"Where else would I be then here? I'm looking for you to spend time with you after you finished work. I thought we had plans for the day."

"Your assistant is in the hospital or with the doctor. Obviously you're worried about her, so why aren't you on your way back there?"

"Let me get this straight. You *want* me to leave? You're actually trying to push me away, back across the country?"

The real question was why did that piss him off so much? After what they'd shared, why was she doing that? Didn't she feel this connection between them growing? Didn't she want this to work between them like he did?

"I'm saying a man who obviously is this worried about an employee should be on his way back to make sure that she is okay. If she was fine and you knew it, you wouldn't be here cursing and looking like you wanted to rip out my window and yell."

"Come with me."

She drew back like he'd reached out and struck her across the face. "What?"

"Come back with me. Meet Wendy, stay at the house for a bit."

Her gaze shuttered and he figured he'd just lost her by asking her to come back with him to meet Wendy.

"I can't just up and leave my work behind, Drew. I have a job that I'm expected to do."

"You're also supposed to be lying low as there's a hit out on you. What better place to do that than in a different country?"

Okay, yes, he was warming up to this idea the longer he thought about it. Get her back to Switzerland with him and go from there. If he had to use Wendy as an excuse, then fine. He had no qualms about doing that. As far as he was concerned, this was war. One he intended to win.

The stiff way she held herself informed him she wasn't as warm to this train of thought as he was.

"So you want me to up and leave my sisters and family who are also in danger, to hide away in a country that hopefully no one will be trying to kill me in?"

"Yes." Andrew held up a hand before she could say anything else. "Let me put it to you like this. If they are trying to find you, perhaps they will leave your family alone."

She crossed her arms. "Or, they will hurt one of them to draw me out, in which case my leaving has only placed them in even more danger."

"Can we at least run it by the detective? It would free up other officers and perhaps they would be able to keep a better eye on the family."

"Let me make this as clear to you as I can. It's not *the* family, it's *my* family. *My* parents, *my* sisters. *My* family."

Andrew shook his head as he stomped into her personal space, forcing her to tip her head back to maintain eye contact with him — as he'd known she would do.

"Let me make *this* clear to you, Tara Lynne Monroe *Coleman*. Your family is my family. We're married and I'll fucking be damned before I allow you to put yourself in unnecessary danger."

"I'm not," she seethed. "I'm doing my job. Which isn't as important to you as yours, I get it. So run along home and make sure your *assistant* is fine."

"Don't start that shit with me again. I've told you that there isn't anything between us. Never has been, never will be."

"Didn't ask because I don't care."

He stepped closer, noting the rapid increase in her breathing along with the pulse in her neck. Canting his head to the side, he gave her a sexy half grin, the kind he knew she loved and couldn't resist.

"When are you going to stop lying about that? You know you care. You know I care about you, too. I'm just

112

waiting for you to admit it out loud. That you love me and want me back in your life."

"I didn't say any such thing."

He put them nose to nose. "You didn't have to, Tara. We may not have been together these past few years, but I still know you. I learned so much about you that short time we were together. I can read your body language."

"Lust isn't even remotely close to love, so if you're reading anything, then it's wrong."

He drifted his gaze to her lips and back up to those incredible black eyes. "Are you sure about that?"

The tip of her tongue peeked out and he groaned, willing his cock to behave.

"Yes." Even with her adamant response, there wasn't any way not to hear the breathiness of the single word that passed her lips.

He leaned closer still until his lips were a hair's breadth away from hers.

"Care to make a wager on it?"

Chapter Ten

Tara inhaled a sharp breath as the plane banked to the left and she spied the amazing display of scenery that came with being in Switzerland. She'd missed it more than she'd believed.

The man across from her appeared to be dozing but she wasn't going to place a wager on that either.

"You okay?" His deep voice rumbled along her skin like heated velvet.

"I'd forgotten how beautiful it is."

"It is one of a kind, that's for sure."

She nodded, watching the snow-capped mountains as they began their descent. About to ask him if he could give her the name of something she'd been thinking about, she cut her gaze to him only to find his eyes locked on her. "You're not even looking at it. How do you know it's so beautiful and one of a kind?"

Those blue eyes burned her and she shifted on the seat.

"I wasn't talking about the scenery. I was talking about you."

Heat flared within her core. Her clit craved just a swipe from his fingers. Or tongue. Then again, so did every other inch of her.

She didn't reply to his comment. Part of her continued to be in shock at the mere fact she'd been convinced to fly with him back to Switzerland. Not just her sisters and parents had been on board, but also her boss. That was the main thing that had her all confused. Why had he been so keen on her heading out? Was she so easily replaced?

"Stop thinking things down that road."

Blinking multiple times in rapid succession, she pulled her focus away from the stunning view and pointed it toward her husband. Also, in her opinion, a stunning view and not at all a hardship to look at.

"What?"

"Why they were all so agreeable to you coming with me. No one wants you gone and no one thinks it's that easy to replace you."

"How do you know what I'm thinking?"

"I told you I know you, Tara. And while I would love to say it's our amazing connection that let me into those thoughts and feelings of yours, you said it out loud."

"That's not exactly fair."

"Never said I would be fair about this. That's not the point, though. The one thing they want, what we *all* want, is for you to be safe."

"My life isn't any more important than that of my family. I would give mine for them."

"We know this. All of us do. But let me ask you this, Tara. How would it make your parents feel to have to bury their middle child? Any of their children?"

"And I'm supposed to be happy about burying them?"

"No. Of course not. But it is the natural progression. We are not supposed to be outlived by our parents. This will be okay. They'll all be fine and ready to see you when you get home. Detective Savvas appears very capable of doing his job."

Tara leaned back in her seat and mulled over his words. He had some valid points and while she could shoot them all down, why do it? Her boss wasn't about to let her back to work right now — he had damn near insisted she take the time. Her caseload was covered and despite her not liking the prosecutor who was taking them, she couldn't argue that they didn't know their job. So what if she found him to be something that had just walked out of the ooze.

Instead of engaging him in further conversation, she leaned back in her chair as they headed for the runway. Tara drew into herself as they landed. She didn't speak as they went from the plane to a waiting car.

As she slid into the back of the running SUV, she scooted all the way to the far door, keeping the middle section open between her and Andrew. The man behind the wheel wasn't one she recognized, but then again, she'd been gone for five years. It made sense for him to have new staff.

Doesn't it?

Christ, she was second and third guessing everything, which she hated with a passion. Clenching her hands into tight fists, she took three deep breaths then forced herself to relax. Although she felt his gaze on her, she refused to glance over in Drew's direction.

Would it even matter? She heard him on the phone, speaking Romansh. He spoke all the languages that were recognized here as national languages but her favorite to hear from him was Romansh. So while she continued to stare out of the window, she sat attuned to his low timbre and the way the words rolled off his tongue.

As they pulled up to the hospital, unease churned with renewed vigor in her gut. And again, she hated it. This was his assistant who was in the hospital. And regardless of whether he was fucking her or not, she hadn't been raised to wish ill on anyone.

Still doesn't mean I want to go in and visit the woman he very well may be having relations with.

She could hear in her mind both Eva's and Shai's admonishing tones. This wasn't proof, and as an ADA she should know so much better than to be thinking that was going to be an issue when he'd told her more than once that he wasn't sleeping with her. Regardless of what the future would hold for them, Drew was her husband and until she had evidence to the contrary, she should be giving him the benefit of the doubt.

The driver held the door for them and as she inched over to his side, Drew reached in a hand to assist her out of the vehicle. She couldn't ignore the warm fuzzies she got from something so simple as touching him.

It wasn't her fault. That was her body's base reaction to the man and there wasn't any force on earth that would get her not to react this way to him. When she tugged on her hand, he didn't release her, only tightened his grip and drew her nearer to his larger form.

They strode through the hospital without any discussion with anyone. Realizing he knew where he was going, she lengthened her diminutive stride so he didn't have to slow down for her anymore.

As they paused before a room, anchored to him as she was him as she was, there wasn't any way to miss the way a shiver ran through him. Concern bypassed her anger and uncertainty and she angled her body into him, offering what silent support she could.

When he met her gaze, she gasped at the amount of uncertainty in his blue eyes. This wasn't the man she was used to seeing nor the one that she wanted to see. Her Drew was confident, unflappable and sure of everything.

"Go on," she whispered.

God, I slept on the flight over and I don't know if he got some bad news about what was going on with her.

His eyes beseeched her, all without him saying a word. Holy fuck, this was breaking her heart. Mustering her courage into a tiny smile, she never dropped his gaze.

"I'm not going anywhere."

That seemed to appease him for he nodded and knocked on the door before entering. He tugged her along behind him, they stepped into the room and she left the door cracked. Every inch of her was asking to remain back, but she forced herself to keep up with him as he approached the bed.

"What the fuck?" His growl was low and vibrated with danger.

Tara peered around him and swore as well. The woman, who would have been a beauty when not covered by bruising and cuts, lay in the hospital bed. Her blonde hair was limp and uneven around her head.

"Go find the doctor, Drew."

"What happened to her?"

Tara swung in front of him, hand against his chest. "Drew. She's sleeping, don't wake her. Go find the doctor and see what information he can provide."

The moment he was out of the door, she picked up the chart. She wasn't a doctor, but her sister was, and she'd picked up a few things over the years, listening to her and visiting her at work. Plus, through her work with the district attorney's office, she had to look over charts on occasion.

So she read it.

Anger built as she realized that this woman had been brutalized. And yet, still all she'd wanted to do was finish his work. That was loyalty. She'd put the chart back down by the time Drew came in.

Tara was sitting quietly beside the bed, staring at the woman, wishing she could take away the pain. Peering up at Drew, she waited for him to say something. Anger clouded his gaze as he stared at Wendy.

In that moment, she realized it wasn't anything other than a platonic affection in his expression for her. Her realization was solidified the second his gaze slid from Wendy to her and heated like the sun's core.

"Well?"

"They can't tell me everything about her condition, but she's been beaten and hit by a vehicle."

"How'd she call you?"

"My guess is she was still on an adrenaline high when that happened. Soon after the phone call ended, she passed out." He scowled and shook his head. "This is my fault."

"How so?"

"Because I left her here to handle this business deal alone. It's a fucking hostile takeover and someone obviously wanted to get their point across. And when I find out who did it—"

"You'll report it to the authorities and allow them to handle it via due process." She didn't alter her tone as the two men walked into the room. Tara recognized *cop* right away. The country didn't matter—cops all had that presence about them.

He snapped his gaze to her before turning around and staring at the men. "What do you want?"

She sighed. This was going to be a long day. Tara was tired, but she also didn't need Drew getting locked up for saying something wrong. Or antagonizing the law.

Andrew listened as the men introduced themselves. Honestly, he didn't give a damn who they were—he wanted to know what they were going to do about what had happened with Wendy. At Tara's suggestion, they stepped out into the hall so they wouldn't disturb Wendy's rest. She reminded him to behave himself with nothing more than a look.

Finally, they left, not giving him any more than he didn't already know from the doctor because it was an active investigation. He scowled. For a moment, he rested his head against the dark door and just struggled to rein in his temper.

Back under control, he pushed into the room. Nothing had changed—Tara still sat by the bed, but she was on her phone, typing something, and Wendy still lay there looking like a broken doll.

Tara looked up and held his gaze. "Okay?"

"No," he snarled in her direction. "How can I be? My assistant is lying there beaten and there's nothing anyone can tell me that the doctor hasn't already. And why isn't she waking up?"

"Hard not to when you're in here bellowing like an enraged bull without any sense."

Wendy's voice reached him and he was beside her in a second. She cracked open her eyes and looked at him, her green eyes cloudy with the effects of her drug drip, but he saw *her* in them.

"If you wanted some time off, Wendy, you could have just put in a request." Andrew tried to keep his tone light for her sake, but inside he wanted to cry and rage.

She gave a weak smile. "I did. It's on your desk."

Andrew cut his eyes to Tara, then back. "I want you to meet my wife."

"Already have. While you were out there talking to the police."

"You didn't tell me she was awake when I walked back in?" He rounded on Tara, who continued to sit in her chair, staring at her phone, not paying him any mind.

"Apparently," she commented without looking up.

He would deal with that later. "What happened, Wendy, and no more hedging. I want to know everything."

Tears sprang to her eyes and she shook her head. "It's not got anything to do with work."

Andrew shook his head. "How do you know this for a fact? You said you were hit by a car."

"I was, but I also know who was driving it."

"And that would be?" Anger and the need for revenge began filling him, an inch at a time.

She shook her head. "I'm not telling you. Because if I do, you'll go do something stupid and halfcocked."

"And why not? You think I'm going to let some asshole treat you like this and stand by doing nothing?"

Andrew could feel Tara's stare boring into him and he didn't look away from Wendy's face. Right now he couldn't handle her disappointment or disbelief in him that there wasn't something romantic between himself and his assistant.

"Let it go."

"Drew."

Okay, he couldn't ignore her now, not when she called his name, even if she was still calling him Drew. Arching an eyebrow, he turned his focus to her.

Tara had risen from the chair and stepped back from the bed. With nothing more than her gaze, she directed him over to stand beside her.

"What?"

"She may not feel comfortable sharing with a man. Especially one who is her boss."

"It's my job to protect her and that's one I failed at. Hell, I failed to protect you as well and you got shot. She got beat and hit by a car."

Tara didn't lose her calm or anything, just reached out and placed a hand on his arm. "Regardless, she may not feel *comfortable* talking to a man. Why don't you go get something to drink from the cafeteria and come back later."

It took him a minute before the words leaving her mouth sank in and he nodded. "Okay."

He walked back to Wendy, bent down and settled a hand on her shoulder. "I'll be right back, okay?"

"I like that she calls you Drew." Wendy's voice was soft and she spoke with care, pushing air by her cracked and bloodied lips.

He squeezed her shoulder and stepped back, looking once more at Tara, who had nothing to show him in her expression. He wasn't sure what to think about that. At all.

During the time away from them, he placed some calls and set up for this final meeting. Now that she was out of the game, he had to do it. There was a secretary, but as he thought about it, he'd not gone to her for anything in years, opting to utilize Wendy instead because, quite frankly, she kicked ass at her job.

Anger still nipped at his heels when he made his way back to the room. Answers. Dammit, he wanted answers.

Pausing outside the door, he was shocked to hear laughter coming from the room. The door wasn't shut all the way and he pushed it open as silently as he could. Tara was seated in the chair beside Wendy, feet up on the cushion, with her chin resting on her knees.

She'd removed her hair from the long braid it had been in and all that black, silky goodness streamed around her lithe frame. Wendy had been moved up a bit in bed but he couldn't see anything of Tara's face. Her back was to him and her hair hid the rest.

"I don't have sisters. I think it would have been nice to have some," Wendy said. "Sounds like the three of you got into some wild situations."

"We're a close family for sure. I have dinner with them at least one time a week and we do a family dinner once a week with our parents."

Wendy yawned and Tara rose. "You should get some more sleep. I'll be back tomorrow, and we'll braid your hair for you, nothing tight but something to keep it out of your face, okay?"

"Thank you. I'm really glad you are fine after being shot."

"And I'm glad you're going to be. You need anything, you have them call for me, all right?"

"I will, but I don't want to be a hassle."

"You're not, but I will not be happy if I learn you needed something and *didn't* call either myself or Drew."

"Understood."

"Good. I'm going to go—I feel him lurking over behind me. I'll see you in the morning." She moved past him. "I'll be outside. Don't stay long, she's exhausted."

Again, Andrew listened to his wife and within fifteen minutes they were on their way home. He drove the cleared roads, sliding on his sunglasses to avoid the glare from the snow. He'd already checked the weather and more was due tonight.

When he turned up the driveway to the home, her sharp intake of breath was music to his ears. Perhaps she had missed this place as much as he knew it had her. He observed her as she climbed out past him once he'd opened the door for her and gazed around.

He walked up behind her and pressed tight to her, one hand splayed against her abdomen, bringing her flush to him and nipped the shell of her ear. "Welcome home, love," he whispered in Romansh.

She didn't reply but she didn't pull away from him. After a bit, he guided her inside the house, needing something to focus on other than her and how much he wanted to strip her naked and push his cock deep inside her. Andrew longed to have her spread out beneath him, hair falling in silken waves on the pristine-white pillows. Except for the one he had under her hips, elevating her that slight amount so he could hit her deeper and make her scream his name, louder and louder with each penetrating stroke.

"Bags are in the bedroom," he said, guiding her to his office.

Her steps grew hesitant as he got them closer to the room.

"What is it, Tara?"

"If you have work to do, go do it. I'd rather not be around if that's what you are needing to focus on, which as there is a takeover attempt occurring, you do have."

"Nope," he said without further explanation.

The moment the door closed behind them with a click, he captured her mouth with his own. Needing her taste to flow over him, embed in him. Remind him there was something in this world he gave a damn about and it was worth fighting for.

With a low purr, she pushed into him. Tara wrapped her arms around him, holding him tighter than she'd done back in her place, and he didn't mind. In fact, he'd love to be held tighter still.

Pushing his tongue deep within her mouth, she whimpered and sucked on it. Her nails began digging into the nape of his neck.

More! His blood pumped, reminding him how much he wanted her. His cock grew swollen and thick, pressing with uncomfortable tightness against the material of his slacks.

Tara didn't wait for anything. She grabbed his belt and unbuckled it. She whisked his zipper down and he moaned in pleasure and need as her small, strong hand closed over him through his boxers.

"Tara," he rasped.

"Talk later," she mumbled.

The second her heated skin curled around his dick, he knew she was right. There wasn't any reason for him to continue to deny what he was looking for and, by all her actions, what she was after as well.

With a low roar, he lifted her and spun them so there was a wall behind her. She slammed against it, eyes widening from the force of his movement. The raw need and desire overflowing in her own gaze let him know she was fine. Hunger was there and his one goal was to feed it.

Mouth devouring hers, he ate all her screams, moans and whimpers as he prevented her from sliding down. She wrapped her amazing, strong legs around him and held him how he wanted. As if she were scared to let him go.

He captured her breasts, using his lower body to keep her aloft. Yes, her legs around him helped but his mind was focused on the spot his cock rested against. Her pussy. He would swear before the Hauge that he could feel her heat pumping into him, egging him on. Encouraging him to continue doing this.

Words escaped him. This wasn't a time for slow lovemaking with his wife. She dug her fingers into his hair and pulled, hard enough that he growled low in the back of his throat and bucked against her. She opened her eyes and nipped his tongue, which elicited another growl from him.

She snapped her perfect white teeth in his direction before kissing him once more. As she kissed, she shrugged out of her button-down, leaving her in the cream bra that covered only part of her breasts and plumped them up like a motherfucking offering that he wasn't about to refuse.

Leaving her mouth wasn't an easy task—he snarled between her lips and this time his mouth clamped over her breast. She moaned and pushed up, allowing him to take in more of the flesh. He twirled it around, grazing the tip with his teeth.

She trembled and purred. His cock pressed with insistence against her. Making love to both breasts, he drew down the silk of her bra, now soaked through, and blew on her exposed nipples. She shuddered.

"Drew." Her breathing came fast and furious. She wasn't screaming his name enough, however. And that was what he wanted.

Chapter Eleven

"Oh fuck yes! Right there, don't you dare fucking stop," Tara cried as Drew took her in the kitchen, hard and fast.

"Never." His growl rolled from his mouth down to dance over her clit, combining with his thumb as he rolled the highly sensitive stiff bud beneath the pad.

His hold on her was proprietary and demanding. She loved every second of it. They'd come down to get a late-night snack. Right now, the ice cream was melting on the counter beside her and the chocolate syrup bottle had fallen to its side, a few drops having spilled onto the marble countertop close enough that her fingers from one hand slipped through it as she held on to any purchase she could find.

Her feet weren't touching the floor and her arms quivered as Drew held her pinned between his heated physique and the cold marble. He powered into her, unrelenting, unending. Fucking perfect.

His blue eyes, so dark they bordered on black, held hers with intense focus. She couldn't look away, even if she'd wanted to. Her throat was raw from all the screaming he'd pulled from her and she'd willingly do it all over again.

"Shit," she rasped, bucking her hips, taking him in as deep as he could be within her. Her body shuddered as she came hard, coating his shaft with her cream.

His teeth were bared in a feral smile as he increased the speed of his thrusts. God, she wanted this every fucking day. Every. Fucking. Day.

She had her entire upper body laid back against the counter, but her arms held her up. He bent down and ran his tongue up from her belly button to the valley between her breasts. When his teeth grazed her taut nipples, she whimpered. When he nipped them, she screamed.

Lips to lips, he drove deep one final time and shot loads of his seed into her. She trembled and purred as he slipped his arms around her and held her tight to the hard planes of his chest. Cock still deep inside her, he carried her back to the bedroom and placed her down on the massive mattress.

His intensity faded and he stared at her in the soft light from the battery-operated candles along the bedside table. Everything about him, with the exception of his body, softened. He took her hands and stretched them out over her head, lacing their fingers together.

Slow and deliberate, he moved within her heat. Withdrawing and pushing ahead once more. Priming all the nerve endings in her core to a nearly unbearable state. Never once did he take his gaze from her.

"Watch me, Tara," he ordered in a soft tone. "I want you to know who's making love to you."

Eyes half-lidded, she tightened her grip on his hands. "I've never had a problem knowing it was you, Drew. Ain't but one man in the world who knows how to make my body sing like this."

"And when I wake up in the morning?"

She arched like a cat, damn near purring as he hit that perfect spot. "I'd say you need to let me sleep because you've kept me up all night."

His grin was fire to her blood. When he broke eye contact and put his mouth down by her ear, she closed her eyes and just gave herself over to the emotions of feeling, living the experience and enjoying every second of the time they got to spend together.

His words were in French this time and she sighed with heavy contentment as he spoke to her. Any of his words were amazing when they fell from his lips in a different language.

* * * *

When she woke after eight, she was alone in the bed but could hear the shower running. After rising, she padded naked to the large closet and opened it. Her mouth dropped open in shock. Her clothes were still there. It was as if she hadn't left.

She reached in and withdrew a robe then slipped it on — the heavy flannel on the inside, silk on the out was one of her favorites. She put on some house slippers then she made her way down to the kitchen and froze once more.

"Mrs. Hilly?"

The housekeeper they'd had when she'd lived there with him was cleaning up the counter where they'd *played* last night. She turned and a smile cracked her weathered face. Mrs. Hilly dropped the rag to the countertop and hurried over to Tara, engulfing her in a hug before she knew what had happened.

"You've come home. Oh, honey, it's so good to see you back here. He's been a complete bear with you gone." She pulled back and smiled again then yanked Tara close once more. "Are you here to stay? You need to be in the house and I would love to have some little kids to clean up after."

That was a phrase that was akin to her being doused in the arctic waters of Greenland. Even so, Tara didn't allow her smile to slip one iota. Instead, she stepped back, fixed it firmly in place and ran a gaze over the woman who'd been so kind to her during her previous stay.

"You're looking wonderful, Mrs. Hilly."

"You are too, a bit skinny. Haven't you been eating?" She waved and shook her head. "I'm thinking you've not been being fed enough." This time there was a hand pat. "That's okay, I'll change that, I'm going to get you all fed."

Just what I don't need is an endless supply of food going in my mouth and landing on my hips.

"I've missed you."

She patted her steel-gray bun and smiled. "I've missed you too. Are you back for good?" Her gaze flitted from Tara to the countertop she'd been cleaning. "From the looks of things, I'd say the two of you are dealing with mended fences."

Tara flushed. Of course she would have found the chocolate sauce, ice cream and other things they'd left lying around.

Mrs. Hilly clucked her tongue. "The Mister and I never played quite like this when he was alive. Makes me wish we had."

Yep, she was officially embarrassed. Tara shook her head and stepped back. When the housekeeper winked at her she smiled in return. A soft chime rang through the house and Mrs. Hilly made her way out of the kitchen, only to return with two policemen in plain clothing — and not the ones from the hospital.

In an instant, Tara was on alert. House visits didn't always bode well for people. Tightening her grip on the robe, she met each of their gazes with aplomb.

"These police officers are asking about Baron Coleman," Mrs. Hilly said.

"He should be in his room or the office, you can go get him." She noticed the way the taller one's gaze flicked between them, following the conversation, and she realized at least one of them knew English. Tara had to provide Mrs. Hilly with a secondary nod before the woman left the room. Even then it wasn't willingly, and she knew that the trip to get Drew wouldn't be long.

They stared at her, one of them being a complete unprofessional in his perusal of her form.

"Why are you here?" The taller one posed the question, and her lip began to curl right away and she struggled to make sure she could get herself under control.

"Why are you here?" She went to the fridge and opened it. As always, there was no shortage of food and she skimmed for the orange juice that she knew was in there for her. No other reason, because he didn't drink it.

"We need to ask some follow-up questions."

"To me?"

"Anyone in the house who is here," the shorter one added, only to clamp his mouth shut when the other cut his gaze at him.

"Here I am. Ask me what you will. I can't tell you much of anything, though. I don't know her that well and haven't been here that long to know anything about the situation."

"Let's start with who you are."

"Tara."

The leering one scanned her again and her skin crawled with the bugs his look left behind.

"You have to have more than that for a name."

"Oh, I do, but I'm not giving it to either of you."

Both drew back as if she'd reached up and smacked their faces. Bushy eyebrows converged on each of the men. Stretching for a glass, she then stood at the island, poured her drink and drank half, all without offering them anything. Never once did her gaze waver from them as she waited.

"Why not?"

"Why should I?"

"We're police."

She dismissed the shorter one and focused on the taller of the two. He came across as the boss. Tara blinked and finished the rest of her juice in silence, never looking away from him.

"How do I know this?"

"Because we told you."

While it had been the second man who spoke, she still didn't look away from the first one. "I've seen no credentials, no badges, no anything to let me know you are who you say you are and I find that incredibly unprofessional for members of law enforcement. Not doing so would make anything, any information I provided you with, unable to be upheld in a court of law."

There came a look of concern on his face. "Not true."

"Wow, now we add in lying and coercion. If you keep down this road, I could have you brought up on charges."

"Who are you again?" The shorter one posed the question.

This time she met and held his gaze for a brief time before slipping it back to the other one. "Assistant District Attorney Baroness Tara Coleman."

"You're an attorney."

"I am, and a damn good one."

"Can you practice over here?"

"No, but I have friends who will co-chair with her." Drew's deep voice was warmth spreading through her like a heated cognac on a cold night. "Ones who work for the ICC."

She whipped her head around to look at him and found his possessive gaze burning into her, not even glancing at the men there.

"I don't appreciate the police coming here and lying to my wife. I think you need to leave and, if you have any questions for us, go through my attorney."

Andrew seethed. How fucking dare they come into his house like that and not only lie to Tara but try to scare her into giving up any information she may have? What about, they hadn't disclosed yet, so he didn't know. Not that it mattered. They'd dared and their superior would hear of this.

Andrew wasn't a member of the peerage, yet barons did have a bit more sway than the average citizen. And he planned on using every inch of his leverage to make them suffer. If it was a demotion or loss of job, he didn't give a damn—they'd bothered *his* wife.

Slipping his gaze from hers, he speared the two men and glared until Mrs. Hilly appeared to lead them from the kitchen and out of the house. Then he focused on the woman standing in nothing more than a robe in his kitchen. Correction, their kitchen.

Perhaps she did have more on than that, but it didn't matter. His mind was focused on the smooth olive skin extending from the bottom of the hem. Needing her close and in his arms to assure himself all was okay with her, he damn near sprinted around the corner of the counter before hauling her up against him and claiming her mouth with his own.

Eyes closed, he savored the taste and feel of the woman along his body. Tiny and fit, she was perfect for him. He lifted her, all the while kissing her as if his life depended on it. In a sense it did.

He couldn't afford to lose her again. Ever so slow after ending their lip exchange, he rested his forehead against hers and once again, opened his eyes.

"Baroness Coleman."

Those two words left him on a whisper and when her eyes widened, he realized she'd been unaware of speaking them. And his mention of it brought it all back.

Andrew wasn't about to let her ignore what she'd announced to everyone who'd been in the kitchen with her earlier. "Yes, you said it. You told two officers that you were Baroness Coleman."

Indecision flashed before she nodded. "Yes I did. It's who I am. Even though I still think it's much better if you let me go, Drew."

"Hell no. I'm not letting you go. Never wanted to, never will." He cupped her face in his large hands.

Fuck, she's so damn delicate and small next to me. I could break her.

And no, it wasn't that he would do so, but the chance was there. Even if he was more careful than ever, she had the potential to be hurt. Perhaps she was correct and he should let her go.

Instant rage flowed. No way. He couldn't live knowing she might turn to another man. If he ever caught one touching her in a personal manner, he would skin the fucker alive.

"I love you, Tara. I was half in love with you when you strolled into my life on that Thailand beach. I know things haven't been good. I want them to be good. I want to learn how to be a good husband for you. I want to learn to be a father for our children."

She cocked an eyebrow. "Children?"

He didn't crack a smile—this wasn't the time for joviality. He had to get her to see how fucking serious he was in regards to this. None of this was the slightest bit funny to him. No jokes. All serious, and if he had to marry her once more so she could understand better, he had absolutely no issue doing that.

"I want a family with you, Tara. I've always wanted children with you. I thought by now we'd have two at least."

"So your plan was for me to stay here after we got married and pop out children for you to portray to everyone, including those at your business, the image of one happy, well-adjusted family?"

"I don't want you to feel like a baby factory so I wouldn't use the word 'pop' but yes, I was hoping to be a dad by now. I won't lie about that. I would love to have a little girl with your eyes or even a son with your expressions and your smarts."

"So, a pretty girl and a smart boy? What about the dog? Do we have one of those?"

He skimmed his thumbs along the smooth skin of her face and gave a slight shake of his head. "I know I'm painting what a lot of people consider the 'ideal' family, Tara. That's not what I'm saying. I don't need the two point five children. I'm saying I want to be a father. I want children. With *you*."

She stared at him and gave a slow nod. "I get it, Drew. Honestly, I do. I know what you mean."

He heaved a sigh of relief to hear that. "Thank you," he remarked, brushing his lips over hers once more. "Do you love me?"

He'd expected her to deny it, change the subject, or any number of things to change the direction of the conversation. Again, he was surprised.

Her gaze filled with a mixture of sadness and acceptance. "I do love you. That time we had in Thailand was unlike anything I've ever had before. You were, and still are, one hell of a person who I see having so much potential to be amazing all the way around." Tara settled her hand against his beard and canted her head to the left. "I didn't want to fall for you. Hell, I didn't want to fall for anyone."

"Glad you didn't fall for just anyone."

His phone rang and he cursed as he dug it out of his pants. "What?"

"This is Dr. Plaleantf and I'm calling about Ms. Triger."

"What happened?"

Tara's expression showcased her own worry as she waited beside him, not moving. She slipped her hand into his.

"She was attacked in the room."

"What?" he roared. "She was attacked? Where was your security?"

"She's asking for you. If you could come down, we'll give you all the answers we can."

"I'm heading in now. And you'd better *pray* nothing else happens to her while I'm on my way." He ended the call and shoved his phone into his pocket.

"Go," Tara said. "I don't need any explanation. Just go."

"I wanted to finish this discussion."

She shook her head. "Wendy needs you."

As he reached for his coat, he searched for any anger or bitterness in the words exiting her mouth. He couldn't find any. So he took her at her word.

"I'll be back as soon as I can."

Tara pushed up on her feet and placed her lips to his. Andrew closed his eyes and savored the connection. "Go," she muttered.

He left the house at a run. Asking his car for as much speed as he dared with the snowy roads, he raced to the hospital. Once he'd parked, he jumped out and ran inside, skipping the lift for the stairs until he reached the floor she was on.

"Baron Coleman, she's still having an MRI. Dr. Plaleantf will see you in his office. I can take you."

A svelte nurse stepped up beside him, her cheerful scrubs not doing a damn thing except pissing him off further, because seeing them meant he was here checking on his personal assistant in the hospital instead of enjoying time with his wife and planning out their future together.

Giving her as much of a grateful smile as he could, he followed her down the hallway into a nice office.

"He'll be right in," she stated, leaving him there.

Andrew didn't sit but paced the back of the room, looking at the pictures and degrees that had been placed about. Not that he cared to see any of them, but it beat sitting there and allowing his mind to race in any and all of the inappropriate directions it was trying to go when it came to Wendy.

It couldn't have been more than five minutes before the door opened once more, but in his mind it had been far longer than it should have been.

"Baron Coleman," the man said, his voice strong but not demeaning.

Swallowing his anger, he turned to watch the man stride in, move around to the chair behind his desk and take a seat.

"Please sit."

"I'm fine," he bit out. "I'd prefer to be told how a patient in your care got attacked in the hospital. Then I want to know who did it so I can go after them." Anger rose and sailed through his veins at the thought of Wendy being hurt not once but twice. And he couldn't help but feel as if this were his fault.

When he left the hospital, with Wendy in the back of the SUV, his mood hadn't improved, but he knew she would be safe with him. The police were after the man who'd managed to come into the hospital and injure her further. Not that it was any consolation to him, but he didn't have the option to go himself. He had to get her back to the house so she would be able to recover there.

Mrs. Hilly met him at the door, her expression one of complete concern as she helped him take Wendy back to a guest room. He left them together to get settled and strode through the large house to find Tara. She wasn't anywhere he could find and as he spun in a circle in their bedroom, he spied a note on the dresser, sitting where he would set any change he had in his pockets at night.

Narrowing his gaze, he reached and plucked it from the surface, opened it and read the words she'd left him. His legs gave out and he hit the carpeted floor with a heavy thump. Tears burned the backs of his eyes as it sank in.

I have two choices. I can let this stick, or I can go fight for my woman and force this confrontation she seems content to ignore.

Chapter Twelve

Tara rested her head against the glass and stared at the scenery that flashed by as the train zipped along the track toward the airport.

I ran again. No, I didn't. I left him a note, which I didn't do last time.

She exhaled and shook her head before settling. The one thing she didn't want to do was spend the entire trip doubting what she'd done. This was for the best. She couldn't wait for his life to calm down — it centered around work. Something she understood, because her life did as well.

How is what I'm doing any different than what I'm accusing him of doing?

She dug her nails into the palms of her hands and tried to slow her breathing. Gazing at her wrist, she checked the time and settled back to do her best to enjoy the view. After all, she was streaking through Switzerland. It was fucking beautiful.

There would be plenty of time on the plane to wallow in self-pity and berate herself for her decisions. Right now, she wanted to relax.

At the airport, she made her way through to her gate and sat there. She had an hour before they even began boarding, so she went in search of some coffee.

Her phone rang and she answered when she saw the name on the screen.

"Hey, Shai."

"When are you getting in? I'll be there to pick you up."

"It's going to be late."

Silence. Tara grinned, picturing her sister just blinking as she stared at her, not willing to give any credence to that sorry excuse.

"I'll text you from Chicago when I'm sure our flight is on time."

"See you do." A moment of silence. "Are you sure you're okay?"

"No. I'm really not but I can't talk about it now or I'm going to start crying." She ordered a coffee and pastry. "The last thing I need to do is scare the entire flight because we both know I'm not pretty when I cry."

"That's true, you're not. For what it's worth, Tara, I'm sorry this didn't work for you."

"You're not going to tell me I need to talk to him?"

"Sweetie, I know I'm pushy, opinionated and a bunch of other things but now, I will not tell you that. I'm your sister and my job is to support you. I may not always agree with what you do but you're a grown, smart, educated woman. There is no doubt in my mind that you have a reason for what you're doing. I'll not say anything until we can sit down and you explain it to me. Just a heads-up, I'm sure Eva will be with me. She's not happy about all of this, so expect a call from her. I have to go. I honestly expected to get your voicemail and I'm in between classes. Love you."

Lord, she missed her family. And she'd not even been over here that long. But they were close. They'd always been there for her and she was used to talking to her siblings a few times a week and seeing them at least twice.

Paying for her drink, she thanked the barista and walked back to her gate. She didn't have anything to bring with her—her suitcase, she checked because she preferred not to have to keep track of it. All she had was her purse.

"Tara Coleman!"

She paused in reclaiming a seat in the gate area at that deep voice who'd just called out her name. Tara longed to convince herself she was hearing things—however, the way her body reacted told her it didn't matter how much, or to whom, she prayed. Drew was there.

How the hell did he find my flight? Okay, so there's probably not that many heading back to my neck of the woods.

With another drink, she pivoted on her heel and found her baron husband stalking through the airport, eyes locked on hers.

Two questions raced through her mind even as she wanted to melt into a puddle from merely looking at all his tall, fine assery. How did he get to her gate? How'd he gotten here at all before her plane left?

Reining in her hormones, she licked her lips and flexed her fingers on her coffee. "Drew."

Thunderheads brewed in his eyes as he bore down on her. People fell silent as he passed, their gazes followed him, anticipation of a public scene the most likely culprit.

"What the fuck is going on? You know, I just about let it go. Said you'd made your decision and decided to run back to fucking Iowa with your tail between your legs. But for some fucking reason I can't just let you go like that. So what's going on, Tara? I thought we had come to an understanding."

She reined in her anger that had been fanned from simmering embers to full-on flames. It had to be controlled—she couldn't yell at him for this because he remained oblivious to the issue.

Enlighten then yell. Damn logic.

Tara blinked and sighed. "Did you? Really, Drew? You thought I would be fine with you telling me I was supposed to stay home and pop out kids because you wanted a family? That because it was in your plans, that's what was to happen?"

A muscle jumped in his cheek and she recognized the sign, that he was working on controlling his own temper.

"I told you, 'pop' was not the word I would have used."

"Fine, I'm to stay home and bear children."

"Yes."

"It's not the eighteen-hundreds, Drew. Women don't have to stay home and run the house while the husband is out."

"You wouldn't have to clean the house, but I'd want you home, yes."

"That's the problem. This is all about you and what you want. Precisely why I said that we never should have married to begin with once I saw how you were after you came back here. Again, not blaming you, because I didn't start the divorce proceedings either. I'd hoped coming here with you would have changed my mind but unfortunately, it didn't. All it did was solidify what I'd thought previously. We need to not be married."

All expression dropped away from his face. "Come on."

"I'm not leaving. I'll be boarding sooner or later."

"Tara. I'm fucking flying you home."

"I've already purchased a ticket, Drew."

"Christ, woman. Let's go. We can get your bag later or have them pull it and send it to the house. And I'll reimburse you for the fucking ticket. I'll fly you there because you and I are finishing this discussion and I don't want to do this where if I turn around you'll run again. You can't run from me if we're in the jet."

She began to shake her head. Okay, private plane was so much nicer than commercial. But he was right that she'd be with him for that complete trip. Was that so wise?

"I'll carry you out of here, Tara." The edge in his tone warned her he was seconds from losing his tenuous hold on any control.

"I can't believe you're doing this. Not exactly behavior for a baron."

He cocked an eyebrow. "Because it's like a baroness to run from her husband when he went to a hospital to check on an employee?"

She ground her jaw and went to his side. Fuming in silence—because he was right, not because she was with him—she listened as he explained to the man at the gate that she wasn't going to be on this flight and they could give the seat away if there was someone on standby, he didn't care. Then he captured her arm in his strong grip and led her away.

Drew didn't speak as they exited the airport, got into a waiting car, headed off to a private strip and boarded their plane.

"Leave as soon as you have clearance," he ordered, still holding her as they went to their seats. He pushed her into a seat and took the one opposite her. "Buckle up."

She listened and held her tongue as they waited for clearance, the taxi, and the takeoff. During the entire time, he never looked away from her, just speared her to the seat with his heated gaze.

"Explain."

The single word fell from his bearded face on a low growl. She skimmed her gaze over him, from the set of his jaw, the hardness in his eyes, the way his large hands gripped the armrests and the absolute rigidity he sat with.

"In everything you spouted earlier—"

"So now you're doubting I even love you?"

She narrowed her eyes at him, not even flinching from the deep bark of his question. "You want me to explain, then sit there with your fucking mouth shut until I get my piece said. Then you can go."

He ran a hand down his beard and nodded.

"Again, in everything you spouted earlier, do you once recall *asking* me what I wanted? Because I don't remember being asked. I recall you talking about how I was going to give up my life and family in the States, to come here and live and provide you kids. That means I am no longer an attorney, well, a practicing one, and I still lose doing what I love. But you do. You can still do what it is you do with your businesses and travel to do all that." She set the coffee down beside her and unbuckled her belt. "And according to you, it's all fine because I won't have to keep the house, there would be a housekeeper. For all I know you're also thinking of having a nanny so I don't even get to be with my children, that I'll bear for you. I have my own hopes and dreams, too, Drew. You're not the only one. And the part that *still* kills me, is I told you them when we first met. Remember that? Back when you actually listened to me!"

She jumped up from the seat and strode to the back of the jet. Drew, right on her heels, spun her around and yanked her in close.

"I want you with me and I want you to be able to travel with me."

"How does that work if I'm having kids? I'm not going to want to travel. And I'm going to resent you for making me give up what I love."

"So you don't love me."

She ignored the pain in his eyes.

"That's not what I said and you know it. But for us, Drew, love isn't going to be enough. I can't just give up the life I fought to make for myself. I'm not going to sit there fat and pregnant while you're gallivanting around the world with your personal assistant who means more to you than you're wanting to admit."

"Fuck this. Do you want me to fire the woman who's made my life so easy the past few years? The one who just got her ass beat again while lying in a hospital bed? Because if that's what you need to feel secure, I will."

Smacking his hands off her, she stepped back. "Yes. I want you to fire her, of course. What woman wants her husband to be with a stunningly beautiful woman, all the damn time?"

"I would hope a woman who trusts her husband wouldn't mind."

"Trust or not, they mind. Even if you fired her, which you can't do, it's not going to change this" — she moved her fingers between them — "thing with us. We can't use Wendy for that. This was there long before she was in the picture."

He threw his hands up. "Jesus Christ, Tara, what do you want from me? I'm willing to get rid of the woman who you have an issue with, you say no. I say you won't have to clean or cook at the house and that's still not good enough for you."

"I want you to fucking listen to me. I *love* being a lawyer. I love working. And if and when I have children, I will raise them, not a nanny. I don't care how many nannies I could have or how much money is just sitting around. I was *raised* by my parents and I'm not letting another person raise mine as long as I'm there and capable. I don't want to give everything up."

"So being with me is giving everything up?"

It was her turn to throw up her hands. "Holy fuck, you're being deliberately obtuse." She stomped over to him and shoved a finger into his chest. "I want to work. I want the man I married to understand that while I don't *have* to work outside the house, I *want* to. I want him to see that this isn't about him controlling every aspect because he wants an image of his family name."

Andrew stood there and listened to his wife's words. This time, he *listened*. He closed his eyes, then snapped them open and picked her up, ignoring her argument, and took them back to the bedroom where he deposited her on the bed. Before she could get up and out of the room, he'd covered her smaller frame with his larger one.

"Listen to me, Tara Coleman."

She pressed her lips tight, forming a small straight line. Her eyes were a bundle of pain and fury. God, what she did to him, it wasn't even fair. Maybe not even be legal in some places. All he knew was that he'd die before he allowed himself to lose this woman. He needed her like he did the air to breathe.

When he didn't immediately speak, wariness crept into her expression. Settling his hand along the side of her face, he brushed his lips over hers before rolling them to the side so they were face to face but he wasn't on top of her.

Pity, because there wasn't a place he loved to be more than that.

"I'm sorry."

She narrowed her eyes and he reached out for her face once again.

"I'm sorry, I wasn't listening to you. I'm sorry I wanted you to be with me with no apparent thought to what you wanted. No, that's not correct, I'm sorry I didn't let you know I was listening, I just didn't let you know *how* I had been thinking and listening. I know I didn't share it with you, but I was thinking of you working when you were here. I was thinking if we could get you into the ICC, then you may consider leaving the States."

Her lips parted in a silent gasp. He inched closer and draped a leg over hers, using the back of his leg to inch her closer to him, putting less space between them.

"Baby, all I want to do is make you happy. I'm not the best at conveying that to you. I thought money and being able to live here would be enough. Then once you were here we could work on the ICC thing. But I forget you weren't raised like me. Family is everything to you."

"You never talk about your family."

"And that's because there's nothing to talk about. I was shipped off to boarding school and raised by the teachers there. My mother is alive and I speak to her maybe once a year. I have a brother and sister who, quite honestly, I have no idea where they are. They've attempted to get in touch with me but that's because they want money." Closer still. He inhaled sharply and allowed the calming scent of cherry blossom and sandalwood to move over him.

"I'm sorry."

"No need to be. It is what it is. I forget that my life isn't how everyone else grew up. And I've met your family. Most of them. The love there is enough to allow the blind to see, it shines so bright. That's what I want, and I'd be lying if I said I wasn't scared about never having it. I *want* that. I want to be part of it. Want to be able to call your parents Mom and Dad. Have hugs from them and your sisters when we see them. To belong."

God, this scared the shit out of him, baring himself like this to her. He had to trust she wasn't going to reach in, rip out his heart and stomp on it while cackling with glee.

It was her turn to touch him and she pushed her fingers through his beard until she caressed his jaw.

"You do belong, Drew. Shai loves you, my parents admire you and I'm sure Eva loves you too—she just doesn't know you yet."

"Tell me you love me."

"I've always loved you, but we need more than that."

"So what do you want me to do? I meant it about Wendy—if you want her gone, I will."

"No, that's foolish and stupid of me. I can't make you do that. I work with guys and you'd have to trust me, so I can't expect any less from myself in that aspect."

"Just for the record, I'm not a fan of you working with men either."

"If you really want to give this a go, are you able to run your work from the States for a while? I mean, could you live with me and still do your job while I see about how we could make this work?"

"I can." His expression sobered. "I would have to bring Wendy over."

"I know. She's not staying with us, though—I draw the line there."

"God, no, I'll get her a small place. She would be at yours often, though, if that's where I am working from."

He knew that wasn't sitting well with her by the way she tensed. Her refusal didn't fall from her lips, though, as he'd expected it to.

"Do what you must."

He took her at her word. Kissing her, he smiled when she purred into his mouth. Rolling them again so she lay beneath him, Andrew decided on making the best of this long flight.

* * * *

Two weeks later, he walked from the car to the front of the apartment building when he froze at the sound of sirens and flashing lights.

What the hell?

A dark blue Crown Vic screeched to a halt near him and the driver's window lowered. He recognized Detective Savvas.

"Get in," the man barked, expression grim. "It's your wife."

Heart at his feet, he bolted for the back door and slid in. He'd barely closed the door when they were screaming off down the street, weaving in and out of traffic like it was standing still.

"What happened?"

"She was shot."

"Again?"

"This is a lot worse than before. She's in surgery right now. I'm not sure of everything. I was sent to pick you up."

He dug for his phone and pulled it out. It had been silenced so he could do his business meeting with his investors. Sourness churned within him.

Praying as they raced along, he swore when he couldn't jump out right away but had to wait for the detective to open the door. The men pounded up the halls until they came to a waiting area containing her entire family.

Tears burned his eyes as Tara's mom hugged him. By the time they got through all of the people there, he wasn't sure they'd not fallen over and run down his face. Andrew found himself seated between Adalyn and Eva, each woman holding his hand. Tight.

His concern was the fact the doctor in the family didn't seem to be all that optimistic.

Did I just get her back to now lose her again? Forever?

God, he hoped not.

Chapter Thirteen

"So you finally found the man who shot my wife?"

Drew's deep voice pushed through the fog surrounding her and she struggled to open her eyes so she could learn who he spoke to.

"We did."

That wasn't a voice she recognized and she fought harder. Everything about her ached. The men speaking faded and when she came to again, the room was quiet. While she was unsure where she was, the one thing she did know, was where she wasn't. This wasn't her bed. It didn't smell of her and it sure didn't smell of her husband. She loved sleeping surrounded by his scent. It made her feel protected and safe.

All of which brought her around to the question she'd been trying to answer. Where was she, where was he, and what the hell was making her so groggy?

It didn't matter. Whenever she tried to pull her shit together and fix it so she could get it all straight, she didn't find the strength and faded.

With a deep breath that hurt, she tried once more. Again nothing but darkness. She couldn't find it to open her eyes.

Maybe the room I'm in is just dark and that's why I can't see anything.

Time and time again, she was lured back by some voices yet still couldn't bring herself to see anything. Frustration mounted, as did her fear that something horrible had happened.

Forcing herself to remain calm, she went through it all in her mind. That at least worked, even if her eyes didn't. She took a deep breath and thought back.

The end of the day couldn't get to her soon enough. There were the days that just flat-out sucked and this was one of them. The judges weren't on her side and none of the cops she had up on the stand said either what she was hoping for them to say or what she expected them to.

She'd gotten into a shouting match with a few detectives and pretty much threatened their careers if they ever pulled a stunt like they had again. Nothing in the way of endearing herself to those men and women who worked hard to bring perps to justice and help her do the same.

When she'd finally been able to stop for lunch, she'd managed to be a klutz about it and drop the entire thing down the front of her suit, staining the cream blouse with yellow and red sauces. All of which called for an outfit change. She did have a replacement in her office, but it wasn't really an outfit she liked, more one she'd been meaning to take home to donate.

Now wasn't the time for that option and she ripped her hose as she shimmied out of one outfit into the other. Dirty clothing in a bag for her to take to the dry cleaners on her way home, she left, hungry, uncomfortable and beyond ready for the day to be over.

It wasn't to be. There was still time for her to be yelled at, her ability as a lawyer questioned and that was just the beginning of her afternoon from hell. Her one lingering bright spot was her dinner with her sisters.

She dropped off the soiled suit, swung home and changed into something far more comfortable for their night out at a local diner. This was one they didn't tend to dress up for and she was perfectly happy in her slacks and long-sleeved Henley. Her sisters were dressed in similar fashion.

The camaraderie and laughter were just what she'd needed and she believed her day of shit to be on the upswing. Right up until they left.

She'd just stepped from the front door with her sisters and made it down to the sidewalk when something cold skated up her spine. Were she a person who believed that she could feel when someone walked on ones grave, this was that precise moment.

Fear exploded up within her and she was frantic, trying to pinpoint where it was coming from. She spied all of the cops who were supposed to be watching them and a few people from work.

Then the slugs tore into her chest. Three of them, catapulting her back through the air. She smashed into Eva, knocking her down as well. As her world faded to black, she saw Shai's mouth moving as others ran into the fading frame.

As it all vanished, she recognized one more person and it all clicked for her then. But it was too late – she couldn't do anything except submerge herself into unconsciousness.

Tears formed and she knew they fell from her eyes as the wetness on her cheeks couldn't be ignored.

A familiar touch skimmed over her skin and she struggled to nestle her face into the calloused palm against her cheek.

"I'm right here, baby. I'm not going anywhere. I need you to come back to me, Tara Lynne." His breath fanned out along her face. "You don't get to tell me you love me then not fight to come back to me. To us."

Drew's voice was shaky, not like the confidence she was used to hearing from him. That alone had her fighting, pushing that tiny bit harder – she needed to reassure him that she was still there. She was fighting. Even though she'd come back to the States, she loved him and always would.

This fighting with him wasn't worth it. They could figure something out. All of it had flashed before her and she didn't want to lose him again. She damn near had. Right now, she wanted to be able to stare and drown in his amazing blue eyes.

Her body wasn't letting her do anything except lie there like a fucking lump on a log.

What the hell is wrong with me? Why can't I open my eyes? Why can't I move? I'm pretty sure I'm not dead. I swear I'm feeling pain. My heart is ripping in two.

She lost the struggle and her world once more faded into nothing.

"Being here isn't doing her a damn bit of good, Shai. We need to get her home. We can afford to have home care for her. This isn't working. She's there but we need her around family and love."

"I think she needs to wake up right now because she's acting like a fucking spoiled brat."

The light hurt her eyes as if a thousand daggers were being shoved into her retinas, but she welcomed it, because as the pain faded and the vision before her cleared, she spied her sisters Eva and Shai standing there by the foot of the bed, staring at each other. Neither of them paid attention to her. Eva held a clipboard in her hand and looked exhausted while Shai — well, she looked a lot like she always did.

"Bitch," she muttered. "How I hate how you look so good no matter what is going on around us."

Both siblings whipped around to face her, mouths open, perfect for fly catching, eyes as big as orbs.

"Tara!"

One on each side of the bed, they hurtled toward her and hugged her. The pain was excruciating but she wouldn't give it up for anything at all. Such a shame she couldn't hug them back.

"You scared the fuck out of us." Eva's words were hard.

"Sorry?"

"We should get the doctor and let Andrew know." Shai kissed her cheek once more and pulled out her phone. "I'll call Drew and send in the doc." She stood, tears in her eyes as she looked down at Tara, gave her another kiss, then strode to the door.

Eva wrapped her tight in her arms and smothered her face with kisses. "I thought we lost you, Tara."

"You saved me, didn't you?"

Her sister had curved partially around her and had her chin resting on Tara's head.

"I did what I could until the paramedics arrived."

"That's a yes." She closed her eyes and welcomed the warmth from her sister. There was no doubt that soon she would be swarmed by many and she wanted to enjoy this. Shai returned with the doctor and both siblings stood back while he performed his necessary tests. As soon as he jotted something on the board, Drew came flying into the room.

His long-sleeved shirt was untucked from his pants, his hair ruffled by what looked like nervous passes from his hands.

"Tara," he gasped, pushing his way to her side.

He cupped her cheeks and kissed her. She closed her eyes once more and allowed his heat to push through her this time. When she opened them again, she found they were alone.

"Hi," she whispered. "I missed you."

His impossibly long lashes rested against his cheekbones for a moment before his gaze locked onto her with the intensity of a missile.

"I can't do this anymore, Tara. I can't lose you like this."

"To be fair, I wasn't planning on getting shot." Her throat was dry and she smacked her lips.

He gave her a small cup and held it while she took a few sips, then he set it away, keeping himself as close as he could to her. Not that she minded—that was something she quite enjoyed.

"I want to yell at you, but I can't."

"I know." She deserved it all and then some, but it would have to wait because her parents came bustling in, and with a final lingering kiss, Drew stepped back to let them in close.

* * * *

Andrew stood on the balcony overlooking the city while Wendy bustled around her new place behind him. He rubbed the back of his neck and shifted his stance. They were working—well, it was more like a break at the moment—but he wanted to leave. Wanted the day to be over so he could head back to Tara.

Not that she was home right now anyway — she was at her physical therapy appointment. He wanted to be there with her, regardless of where she was.

He still woke with night sweats about her being shot and almost taken from him. Tara had withdrawn somewhat and he didn't like it. But he did understand.

She'd come very close to death this time. Much closer than the previous time she'd been shot. Exhaling sharply, he spun on his heels and stepped back inside, where it was warm. Winter had lingered and he was ready for something a bit warmer, were he honest.

"All good here, boss."

Forcing a smile, he nodded at Wendy. Not that he didn't want to smile around her, but he had other things on his mind. She looked so much better now that she'd been over here for a while. The bruising and cuts on her face had faded, she'd put on weight, not looking so anorexic, and the exhaustion was gone from her eyes.

"Thanks, Wendy. Now, you are coming tonight for dinner, right? I'll have a car here to pick you up at seven." He moved through her place toward the front door, not really waiting for an answer.

"Of course. Thank you for inviting me."

There was a slight shiver at the end of her statement that slowed his exit. With a pivot, he returned to her side and gripped her arms.

"You're family, Wendy. Tonight is a family dinner."

She wouldn't hold his gaze but lowered hers to look elsewhere. "Regardless, thank you."

He kissed her forehead and left, heading down to the car waiting for him. He scrolled through his phone and pulled up Tara's number then called her.

"I'm just now done," she said by way of greeting.

"I'll be there shortly to get you."

"I don't need you to drive me all over town. Correction, have your car service do it."

"Indulge me."

"I've been doing a lot of that lately."

He smiled. She had for sure. Most of the time that happened when it was just the two of them. His cock swelled and pushed hard against the seam of his slacks.

"Don't hear me complaining about that, do you?" Her utterance wasn't flattering so he ignored it. "I'll see you soon."

She sat outside on a bench that he had no doubt was a stunning spot to be in any season, aside from the lingering winter upon them. The moment the car halted, he jumped out to meet her.

As he strode over the shoveled walkway, he smiled in her direction. This little sprite of a woman didn't look at all like the one he'd seen eat people alive in court. Or the saucy vixen who was a devil in his bed as she made him come apart, or as he watched her fall to pieces.

No, this one was cute. Her neon-green knit cap with the pompom on the top and ear flaps with pink stars on them just made him laugh. She didn't even move — hell, he wasn't sure she knew he'd arrived. Her nose was in a book.

Not on her phone or an e-reader but an actual book. When he stood over her, she used a mittened hand to slide a piece of play money in as a bookmark. Only then did she look up at him with her black eyes.

"Hi."

He bent and kissed her, savoring the smoothness of her gloss beneath his own lips.

"I missed you. Ready? And why are you sitting out here in the cold?"

"I'm not cold. Yes I am."

He offered her his arm and helped her up. She was still a bit off balance but had come along much quicker than they'd expected her to. Tara wanted to quit therapy, but he and Eva had nixed that idea.

Once in the heated vehicle and on their way, he reached over and tucked some wayward hair back from her eyes.

"How do you feel?"

"Well enough for dinner. I told you, I'm fine. I tell you and Eva this all the time, but you expect me to continue going to therapy. How's Wendy? Is she coming tonight?"

"I won't stop expecting you to go. Yes, she is. She thinks it's just family dinner and doesn't have a clue it's a birthday party for her. I told her I'd have the car by to pick her up. You sure Shai is up for this?"

"She is. We confirmed earlier today with her. All is ready for tonight. She'll take care of anything last minute with Mom."

He stroked her cheek with his thumb. At least now he wasn't concerned about her and her beliefs on what was going on with him and Wendy. It hadn't been an easy road. They still had one more hurdle to get over, though, and that was one he knew would be coming soon.

"What's got that pensive look on your face?"

He put his gaze back to her from where it had drifted outside the car. "Work."

"Everything okay there?"

He nodded. "Wendy is a gem, she could run it all without me. Thank God she doesn't want to." He grinned. "Or at least doesn't know she could."

"Trust me, she knows." Tara leaned against him with a yawn. "That woman definitely knows."

"I've got some people looking to poach her from me."

"I don't think you have anything to worry about. You pay her well, although you may want to see about a raise, and from what I see, treat her nice. At least now you do."

He took the jab without offense, because she had the right of it. He'd taken her for granted all the way up until Tara had gotten back in his life. Now he saw how valuable Wendy was to him on more than one level.

Back at her place, he walked her into the large bathroom and began disrobing her.

She watched him with heavy-lidded eyes, not helping him but not stopping him either. Layer by layer she was exposed to him until she was naked before his hungry gaze.

On his knees before her, he looked up at the woman he loved more than he'd ever be able to put into actual words. Petite everywhere but perfect for him. To him. His heart caught as he stared at the scars left behind from the bullets that had penetrated her olive skin and come so close to taking her from him. Permanently.

She canted her head to the side. "I know that look. You've pensive. What's rattling around up there?"

"Just thankful I still have you here with me." He reached out and touched the puckered skin in her chest area. Dropping his head so she wouldn't see the tears burning him, he rested it against her stomach.

She pushed a hand into his hair and threaded it as she comforted him.

"Drew, I have to shower."

There it was. Her closing the door on that talk that still lingered. That final hurdle for them.

Kissing his way up her skin, he rose as he captured her mouth. As the kiss deepened, he kicked off his shoes, toed off his socks and rid himself of his pants and underwear. Breaking for a moment, he ripped his shirt off over his head then reclaimed her mouth beneath his own.

She purred as she arched into him. Andrew lifted her, smiling against her mouth as she wrapped her legs about him. The kiss continued as he waited for the water to heat. His cock, hard and throbbing, rested against her core and he could feel her wetness, slipping up his shaft.

God, he loved this woman.

When the water was warm enough, he put them both under the spray. She pulled on his hair as the kiss intensified. Palming one breast, he teased it until the nipple was a hard pebble in his hand. He trailed kisses down her neck until he could capture her other breast. Plucking the tip of one and tonguing the other, he had her squirming in his embrace.

"Drew," she wailed. "Stop this. Please, I need you inside me. We don't have time for this."

Grazing his teeth along the point, he mumbled, "There's always time for this between us, Tara."

"Inside me," she demanded.

He didn't want to wait any longer and lifted her enough so the head of his cock sat poised at her core's entrance. Then he released his hold on her, allowing gravity and her own weight to take him in.

"Yes," she hissed as he filled her.

He didn't have another word for it. Her velvet walls tightened around him and when she flexed, sweat broke out on his skin only to be whisked away by the falling water. Holding on, he gave them both what was needed. Each other.

Chapter Fourteen

"Here's to the lucky bride-to-be." Shai raised her martini glass, a smile set in place.

Tara mimicked the action with her glass of Chardonnay. She was out with her sisters and Eva had told her that she and Grant were engaged. "I second that. I'm so happy for you. And let's look at this honking ring you've got there."

Eva blushed as she looked at the ring and her sisters. "I never thought this would happen. Thank you for being excited with me."

Tara grinned. "Why wouldn't we be? This man makes you glow."

Eva cocked an eyebrow. "Speaking of glowing," she said, giving Tara a pointed look.

She held up her hands. "Nope, my life is off limits tonight. This is about you and Grant. And you again. We're here to celebrate what you two have. Shai? Back me on this."

Her sister waved for another drink. "Absolutely. We'll talk about her glow later on—right now, this is about you."

"Excuse me, ladies, I'm sorry to interrupt."

Tara's heart jumped at the sight of Detective Savvas.

"You have news on Veronica?"

Her chest hurt and she struggled not to rub it in front of this man. It wasn't his fault her own secretary had been the one to pull the trigger this last time, but seeing him was bringing it all back.

From his expression, he knew he wasn't helping anything.

"We've heard from sources that she is back in town."

Eva took her hand and Tara breathed a bit easier.

"And have you heard *where* she is?" Shai snapped.

Savvas flicked his gaze to Shai. "Not yet. We want you to be aware. We do have people on you again."

"Fat lot of good it did last time."

"Ms. Monroe, we are doing our best to keep her and the rest of you safe. I'm sure that someone will be by tomorrow to inform you, but as I saw you while I was leaving, I wanted to let you know."

"If you were paid for your performance, I'd go with you're being overpaid."

"Shai," Tara reprimanded.

Detective Savvas didn't look at all put out by her sister's attitude. A small smile turned up his lips.

"I assure you, Ms. Monroe, I earn every penny I make with my performance. I hope you ladies have a good night." He strode off without a look back.

"What was that about, Shai?" Tara shared a glance with Eva.

"What? They were supposed to be protecting you last time and look what happened. Forgive me if I don't think that he's doing the best job he can."

"To be fair, he wasn't the one protecting me. I'm sure he's very capable."

Shai shrugged and accepted her new drink before downing a good chunk of it at once. "Enough about that. Let's get back to the celebration. And I want cake, who's with me?"

Tara nodded. "I spend enough time dying on that goddamn bike in spin class, I can have some too."

Eva picked up the dessert menu. "Someone try and stop me."

"Hell no, you'll probably kill me for even thinking it. I know you love your sweets."

They celebrated into the night and, with hugs, finally separated and went their own ways home.

Unease settled around her as she drove. Every set of headlights was a potential assailant. Her mind didn't help matters either.

What if they've tampered with my vehicle? What if once I reach a certain speed on the interstate I trigger the bomb and it will go off the moment I decelerate, like it did in the movie? What if someone has hacked my GPS and they have some control over my car, telling it where to go and they wreck me?

Her palpitations were out of control as she made it to her parking place at her building. Shaking, she couldn't make her fingers work to get out of the vehicle.

Fumbling, she called Drew.

"Hey, sexy, how is your time with your sisters?"

"I'm in my car downstairs and I can't make my hands work." Tears burst from her eyes and she began dry heaving. Only, after a few moments it wasn't just dry heaves.

"I'm on my way. Stay on the line with me, baby."

In the back of her mind, she could hear his footsteps as he ran through the apartment. There wasn't a ding from the elevator and when he burst from the stairwell, she realized why. He'd run down.

Drew wore nothing but jeans and shoes. He skidded to a stop by the driver's door and hung up the phone. She rocked, fingers clutched around the wheel.

"Baby," he said through the glass. "I need you to unlock the door."

Nodding, she took a minute to accomplish that. Seconds later, his heat surrounded her, and she inhaled deep, allowing it to sink in as best it could. He undid her belt, and keeping her tight to his chest, he backed away, carrying her with him.

He handed her the purse and shut the door with his hip before walking to the elevator, strong arms anchoring her to him. She closed her eyes and allowed the tears to fall—she didn't have the energy to stop them.

Silence lingered between them as they rode up to her floor and into the space. He didn't stop in the living room, just continued on to the bedroom where he placed her on the bed. Drew wedged himself between her thighs and cupped her face.

"Baby, look at me."

Shame washed over her and she shook her head. "I don't know what came over me. I shouldn't have been scared but I freaked out." Her breaths came sharp and ragged. "All I could think about was that they'd tampered with my car with the GPS or a bomb and I was going to die. Headlights scared the shit out of me and I think I threw up in my car."

"You're safe, it's okay." He tucked her into him and rubbed her back.

She fell asleep after he made her drink a warm cup of tea and held her on his lap for a while. She woke the same way, curled up against him. Only this time they were naked and in bed.

"Drew?"

"Right here, baby." His large hand moved in idyllic patterns along her back. "I'm right here. Do you need me to get you something? A drink? Food?"

"No," she blurted out, fingers tightened on his arm. "Stay with me. Please."

"I'm not going anywhere."

She settled into him a bit more, calming her racing heart and willing her breathing to slow down. Her husband didn't speak—he just remained there, touching her. Offering support all in silence.

She dozed off and on until she could no longer ignore her screaming bladder. With a frustrated groan, she untangled herself from his warm, hard body and padded along the thick carpet to the spacious bathroom.

Once she'd finished, she rested her just-washed hands against the porcelain sink and stared at her reflection. Bags lingered under eyes and her features appeared a bit drawn.

Standing tall, she peered at the scarring on her chest and moved her fingers so she could trace along the edges. She flinched upon first contact. Not because it hurt, but because she was expecting it to. As she worried her lower lip in her teeth, she continued her exploration of the scars.

Nothing else mattered, not that she stood there naked before the mirror, not that she was exhausted, just the reminder that would be with her forever, because of her job.

"Tara?"

She cut her eyes toward the door. "Yes?"

"Everything okay in there?"

"Just staring at my scars." Canting her head to the side, she poked at the puckered edge once more.

When the door opened, she didn't jump in shock, didn't even take her gaze from where her fingers rested. His large body moved up behind her, sharing his warmth with her nakedness.

"I almost died."

"I know." He cupped her shoulders and she allowed her gaze to flick to the clean square nails on the ends of each finger.

"I shouldn't have these panic attacks."

"Why not?" Drew's question wasn't snide but just curious.

"Because I'm an ADA and I should know better."

Drew shook his head and swept her up in his arms. "We need to have a talk and now is the time."

Swiping her robe on the way out of the bedroom, he then set it around her shoulders after he put her on the floor in the living room.

"Sit."

She arched an eyebrow, but he didn't budge, just pointed down to the large sofa.

When she complied and tucked her legs beneath her, he reached over to drag the quilt off the back and settled it around her, tucking it in.

He didn't sit beside her — instead, he propped his ass on the coffee table and leaned close to her.

"I wanted to wait for this until you were better, but I'm thinking this is pertinent to talk about now."

The Tara he knew and had fallen for would've watched him with a sparkle and slight challenge in her eyes. Waiting for him to say what he had to say so she could either counter with her own well-planned argument, or one that she thought would hold merit just because she loved to debate. However, this one, this version of his wife, merely sat there, her eyes affixed to his as she waited.

The robe and the quilt surrounding her made her appear even smaller, more petite. Even more fragile. What it did was bring out more of his protective instincts, making him want to sweep her up and carry her all the way back over to Switzerland where he could keep her safe and away from everything that went on in this crazy world of hers.

That wasn't an option, though. She wasn't the kind of woman who would run and hide from anything, no matter how scared she got. And he understood she was scared. The call he'd received from her had torn out his heart and dropped it down to the street level.

When he'd gotten out there and seen her drawn face and pale skin he'd damn near panicked. This was not the woman he knew. But now, having watched her stare at her own scarring and talk about the near-death experience that she'd just gone through, he accepted they had to have this discussion now.

He had to know where everything was laid out.

He blinked and focused back on her face. She hadn't fidgeted or given him any one of her numerous patented 'I'm bored and still waiting' looks.

"This thing that you went through, Tara. There's no timeframe for you to be healed from it. No time that anyone is going to say you should have moved on, shouldn't let what happened to you worry you any further. I need you to understand that. You heal at your own rate. You work through this at your own speed. If it takes you a day, fine, if it takes you ten years, fine. I don't care. All I care about is you getting better."

She began to shake her head and he reached out, capturing her chin, holding it in place.

"No. I know I said discussion, but right now this is going to be a very one-sided one. I want to talk and I want you to listen."

She nodded. Not much of a movement, but from this woman he would take it.

"I've gone back and forth in my head about how I want this to play out between us. I've told you how much I love you and I know you told me the same thing." He pushed a hand through his hair before rubbing his palm on the material of his pant leg. "Seeing you like this is breaking my heart. Hearing you doubt the amazing woman that I know you are. That your family knows you are. All of this kills me a little more each time I'm faced with it."

Andrew reached over and removed one of her hands from the folds of the quilt that covered her before lacing their fingers together and skimming his thumb along the side of her palm. Such strength resided within this hand, regardless of how tiny it was in his own.

"When I first met you, on the beach in Thailand, right away your energy, zest for life reached out across the sand and snared me. It dug into my skin, my heart. My *soul*. And I was okay with that, because I never wanted to let you go."

He flashed back to the day they'd met and once again saw the sun shining on her glossy black hair. The streak of pink faded, not as prominent as it was now, however just as attractive.

"It went beyond the physical for me, Tara. From the very beginning I've always known you were the one for me."

Tara shifted on the couch, not so much getting away from him as getting comfortable. He waited until she settled once more.

"I didn't want to tell you I was a baron, because I wanted you to like me for me. I wanted you to love me for the man you met standing in horrible print short swimsuit trunks, flip-flops that had definitely seen better days and a baseball cap that never even made it home from the island."

"I'm sure the boy you gave it to is still proudly wearing his hat." She shrugged a little and gave him a slight smile.

"I hope so. But I don't want to talk about him. You told me before that when we got back to Switzerland I changed. I can't deny that I did, I agree, I put away the fun-loving, jovial man who'd fallen in love and replaced him with the cold, straight-laced businessman."

Shit. This was so much harder than he'd thought it was going to be. Baring ones soul to another was as difficult. It shouldn't have been — he should be able to spill and she would listen then talk. And they could move on.

So not how this was going down.

"I quite honestly thought at that point, that once you found out I was a baron and you didn't have to work, you would've been happy with that and would've stayed just because. I mean, what woman wouldn't want to be able to do whatever she wanted without ever having to worry about work again?" Andrew shifted on the coffee table, sliding his feet beneath the sofa.

"Then I came home from work that day and you were gone. My entire world crashed down around me. After you just headed home as you said you needed to, I figured you would be back relatively quickly. With that knowledge I dove back into my job once more. But you never came home."

Christ, he needed a drink. Something old and aged with a fine smooth finish would be preferable.

"Once Wendy found out about you, she made it her mission to keep tabs on you. She followed you constantly, always letting me know what was going on, when you got shot the first time, when you won big cases. All of it. She let me know. And I was grateful, because it was a way I could keep you in my life without actually having to face the fact that you had left me. That my wife had walked out on our marriage."

Tara lowered her gaze and he allowed it for a few moments before reaching out tipping her chin up until their eyes met once more.

"Are you ever going to leave the District Attorney's Office? I know your dream is to be part of the ICC, but would you leave for anything other than that?"

Tara didn't say anything. Her unflinching black gaze stared straight through him, peering at his soul, unraveling each layer one at a time, exposing him more and more as the clock ticked each second away.

"Tara?"

"I didn't think so for the longest time. I mean, this is my home. I grew up, here went to school here, and my family is here. It would have to be a pretty strong reason for me to leave."

His heart fell. If that was what she was thinking now, there was no point in him continuing on. Perhaps he could keep some of his dignity intact and not confide everything to her before she stomped on it and ground it to pulp, left to be blown away by the first wind that came along.

"I have to get back to Switzerland."

Andrew swore in his mind when not a single expression moved across her face at his words. *Do I mean so little to her that the prospect of me leaving permanently doesn't even warrant a slight eye widening?*

"I thought you just got Wendy settled. Why do you need to go back now?"

A seed of hope cracked open within the pit of his belly. Perhaps, just perhaps she wasn't as cold as she was pretending to be toward him at this moment.

"I can't stay here and watch you get hurt. Watching you turn down the protection that I offer. This is killing me, and short of forcing you to come back with me I don't know a way to keep you safe."

Her eyes narrowed and he tensed.

"Is that what this is all about? You feeling the need to run because I've been getting shot? Because I had a breakdown after I'm told that they find out the woman who shot me is back in town. Because of that you now feel the need to—"

"Wait a second! What the fuck are you talking about? That bitch is back in town? And she's not in custody?" Fury pulsed through his veins with each beat of his heart.

"Not from what I was told. So I'm sorry that you are feeling inadequate and you need to head home because you can't stand watch me be in this situation. Perhaps you're right and it is better that you leave." She closed her eyes only to have them fly open once more. "You can take the bed, I'll be fine here on the couch."

As she rolled away from him, his heart went with her.

Chapter Fifteen

"Tara? Tara? Tara Lynne, are you even listening to me?"

Pivoting, she stared at her mother and gave a slight shake of her head along with a wry grin. "No, sorry. I was lost in thought."

"Any idiot can see that. What's going on with you? And don't tell me nothing because I'm your mother and I know when you're lying to me. In regards to most things."

Tara didn't even comment on that, well aware her mother was referring back to the fact she hadn't told them about her marrying Andrew.

"I'm just lost in the roads of my own mind."

"Really? I would've thought it something along the lines of your husband's about to leave you and head back to Switzerland. You're trying to figure out how to break it to me that you want to go with him but you also don't want to lose everything that you've done for yourself here in the District Attorney's Office. Am I warm?"

Tara knew her mouth had to be open wide enough for a colony of bees to set up shop. Her mother just laughed, albeit a bit sadly.

"How did you even—" She clamped her mouth shut when her mother waved a hand.

"Baby girl, I've been married for a good number of years, been in love for longer than that and have known you almost your entire life."

Adalyn Monroe wiped her hands off on the towel draped over her shoulder as she approached her middle daughter. The woman was still a knockout.

"I don't want him to think I'm just going with him because he makes it so I don't have to work at all if I don't want to." Tears of frustration burned the corners of her eyes and she furiously blinked them away, determined not to let them fall.

"What makes you think he's gonna say that? Or even think that? That man loves you. I don't know any other way to describe it."

"I just can't seem to say or do anything right around him. I've been so focused on me, what could possibly happen to me or you, Eva, dad, Grant or Shai. For so many years it's just been easier to pretend it doesn't exist and not to have to think about his feelings and how my actions may hurt him." The first hot tears splashed down her face and her mother wiped them away, her expression soft.

"Tara Lynne, marriage is hard work. Bone-breaking, sweat-making hard work. It's not something that works just because, this is something that works because both parties involved fight to make it work. There are good times, lots of them." She brushed some hair away from her face. "Like how you feel the baby in your arms for the first time. How you feel on those Sunday mornings when you can stay curled up in bed and listen to either the rain or even just the birds and know that *he* is the one that *you* chose to be with."

Tara wanted that. She wanted all of that with him.

"He's gonna leave. He's taking Wendy and they are going back."

"And when is this happening?"

She shook her head. "I don't know."

Her mother huffed and Tara scrunched her face as she looked up at her.

"Let me ask you something. I want you to be completely honest with me and yourself."

Tara stared at her mother searching for him to joke or laugh, only to come up empty. "Okay."

"Right now, if it came down to it, a choice between staying in your apartment and working at the District Attorney's Office or being with your husband, regardless of where he is going to be. Which would you choose?"

She had to swallow back her initial response of staying and doing what she was doing now because she'd conditioned herself long ago to give that answer. Conditioned herself to forget about the man that she had left behind.

Her mother didn't rush her. She just sat there and stared, waiting with maternal patience Tara wasn't ever sure she'd had or would have even if she had her own kids.

"I'd go with him."

Just saying the words released the pressure on her chest and the weight bearing down on her shoulders, and her soul seemed to weigh nothing at all.

"Are you sure about that?" Tara nodded. "Then go tell him."

Mrs. Monroe kissed her on the cheek, stepped back and watched as she put on her coat, escorted her to the door, waved to her middle child before she drove out of the driveway, headed off toward her destiny.

Drew wasn't at her apartment when she got there, and she tried not to panic because, when she'd run the first time—okay, both times—she'd left her clothes.

Digging her phone out of her purse, Tara pulled up his number and punched the dial button. She paced while she waited for him to pick up.

"Baron Coleman's phone."

Wendy.

"Hi, Wendy, it's Tara. Is he available?"

"Not at the moment, no. He's on a conference call. Would you like me to take a message?"

Tara wanted to reach through the phone and punch her for answering her husband's phone, even though she understood why she did and she trusted that there was nothing romantic between the two of them. It still gnawed at her gut.

"No message necessary. I can just swing by and drop something off for him."

"My best guess is yes he will be here for a while. He ordered dinner a little bit ago and that hasn't arrived yet. Would you like me to order something for you? That way you could eat dinner together?"

"What a sweet offer, but that's okay. Thank you, though. I have no desire to interrupt his busy schedule so I will simply swing by. I'll be fast and will get back out of your way."

Wendy chuckled. "Please, I know he'd much rather see you and spend time with you than deal with the people he's on the phone with. Would you like me to tell him you're coming?"

"Not necessary. I'll be there shortly, and thank you, Wendy."

Tara took a quick shower and, while she dried, sat down in front of her computer to type up a letter. Once she had dressed and was ready to go, she headed down to her vehicle and drove off toward Wendy's.

Pulling into the apartment lot, Tara gazed around, her nerves ratcheting up with each passing second. This was the perfect place for someone to take another shot at her, or do something to her vehicle. Her palms began to sweat. She struggled to breathe and regain control.

Giving herself the five minutes she needed, she climbed out of the vehicle and locked the door before heading inside. Her back was covered in slick sweat, making her feel as if she'd yet to take a shower at all. The building was more of an old warehouse that had been converted into large, single-floor studio-style apartments.

She stepped into the lift and drew down the metal gate before pressing the button to take her up to the third floor. Once there, she opened the door and raised the gate before stepping out. One more deep breath and she was on her way to Wendy's door.

A final touch to her face to ensure she wasn't still sweating like a stuck pig, and Tara reached out to knock. Seconds later the door swung open, leaving her face-to-face with the tall, beautiful blonde who went by the name of Wendy.

"Some days I hate how beautiful you are," Tara blurted out before slapping a hand over her mouth and staring up at Wendy, eyes wide as a mixture of shame and shock rolled through her.

Wendy smiled, showing off her perfect teeth as she waved her into the space. "I think that's one of the nicest things anyone has said to me, although I'm not sure why you would hate me for it. I look positively dowdy standing next to you."

Tara shook her head. "Not even close."

Wendy's smile never faded. She gestured toward the back and said, "He's over there. Fair warning, he's in a mood. In a serious mood. And on that note, I'm going to step back to my bedroom and see if I can get some work done. Yell if you need me."

After a quick check to make sure the door had been locked behind her, Tara strolled through the spacious place, her heels clicking on the wood floor, and headed back to where her husband was. His back was to her as she approached. His deep voice rolled over her, plucking her strings as if he were the only one who knew her secrets. And he was.

"I don't care if you offered me three million, I'm not selling you that piece of property when I know exactly what you're going to do with it." Drew shoved a hand through his hair as he shook his head. "What difference does it make to you if I take it as a loss? The property will be saved and the people who are living there won't have to go on and find a new place to live just because you want to throw up some high-priced place for your friends to stay."

Her heart warmed as she heard those words. Drew truly was a wonderful man.

Moving up behind him, she slid her hands over his shoulders, smiling as he leaned back into her touch.

"With that, we're done with this conversation." He touched his ear and effectively cut off communication before pulling out the Bluetooth earpiece and dropping it on the desk. Then he rested his hand on top of hers and said, "I told you, Wendy, not like this, my wife could stop by at any moment."

Tara wanted to be mad, wanted to yell at him for that, but she couldn't, given the way his shoulders were shaking as he tried to contain his laughter. He dipped his head back and looked at her, all the love in his eyes, and it warmed her all the way through.

"Very funny."

"I thought so. What are you doing here? Is everything okay?"

He captured her hand in his, pulled her around and brought her to stand between his open legs. With a quick kiss to the back of her hand, he released her and settled his touch upon her hips.

She didn't think so. In that moment, standing there with him, she realized that how things were at this moment were not okay. It was not what she wanted and, like her mother had finally gotten her to admit, it was time to change that.

"No."

The moment the word no had passed her lips, he wanted to bolt up from the chair and demand she tell him what the problem was so he could go out and fix it. After all, that was his job. Take care of this woman, love her, protect her, and make her feel safe. Something wasn't right. His task was to fix it.

Or so he'd thought. Until he'd come to the realization that she would always pick her career over him. So he stayed seated and watched her expression.

"What's going on?"

Yep, he'd got that right. Some interest, yet not a complete investment, as if his entire world hinged on the words coming out of her mouth.

"You're different."

Andrew shrugged in confusion. He wasn't sure where this conversation was headed and, if he were to be honest, he wasn't entirely sure he wanted to know.

"Different how and compared to what?"

"Different from last night. Your eyes, they've changed."

Andrew sighed and sat straighter so he was closer to her. "I know you didn't come all the way over here because my eyes are different than they were last night. Talk to me, Tara."

Good job. No begging for her to let me help. I can be the strong one. I got this.

Not even he was buying his mental pep talk. Ignoring it for the moment, he retained his focus on his wife.

"I was thinking about what you said last night."

And there it was. His stomach plummeted to the soles of his shoes and he swallowed back the bile that threatened to escape.

"Perhaps we should discuss this later." She shook her head. "Or perhaps now would be better."

Way to be strong, jackass.

"I know you have to leave. I mean, I know you're planning on leaving and heading back to Switzerland." She swallowed and looked everywhere but his face.

Interesting.

"As you haven't told me when you're leaving, I didn't want to risk missing you flying away and not being able to tell you what I really need to say."

"What the hell do you mean you're moving back to Switzerland? You drag my ass all the way over here, make me go through what I had to go through to get a goddamn work visa and now you're telling me we're heading back to Switzerland? When were you planning on telling me this? Or were you thinking you were just going to leave me here and head back without me?"

Wendy's sharp voice broke through their bubble and they both turned to look at her striding up, jaw in a set line. She glared between the both of them and Andrew almost stepped in front of Tara out of his instinctive need to protect her.

"Can we not do this now, Wendy?"

"No. I mean I understand that you two have issues to work out but I need to know if I'm supposed to be packing" — she gestured around the loft — "all of this in preparation to fly home."

Andrew sighed. He'd not told her anything, and by her he meant Wendy, because he didn't want to leave the woman he'd married.

"Wendy, please. Give us a minute."

"Fucking uproot my life and drag me across the world then uproot me again all without any notice, or even buying me dinner first."

"Wendy," he warned.

She swore and whirled around, stomping off. "Can't even be in my own damn place without yet another man giving me orders and deciding my fate."

He rose and lifted Tara with him, even as he turned to follow Wendy with his gaze. His fingertips burned with the need to touch the woman he held.

Why does my life have to get so bloody complicated?

He slid her down his hard length until she had her feet again on the floor. "Tara."

"You want me to wait?" His wife posed the question in a hushed tone.

God no. Then again, yes. He did. Forever. He wanted her to wait forever to be with him. At the same time, he wanted to spend this time with her and figure out what it was that had driven her to come find him here.

"I should go explain this to her."

Again, that expression of hers wasn't anything he could read and it bugged the shit out of him. While it may have been amazing for court, it sucked for him to try and get a bead on her emotions.

He swore she withdrew into herself a bit before she nodded. "Go, do what you must. I should get going. I had only planned on being here for a short bit. If you need to talk to her, I can head out."

"You just asked me if you should wait." He scratched his jaw. "I want you to wait."

"I'll be better letting the two of you deal with this here. It's her place and I was wrong coming here to make her have to listen to anything between us."

"You're basically telling me if I go talk to her, you're not going to be here when I'm finished."

"I'm telling you that I will head home and be there when you're done here. I do apologize for interrupting your day." Her tongue swiped along the seam of her lips and he longed to take the time to follow it with his own.

"Tara," he groaned.

A smile came but he knew she could tell it was forced.

"I'll see you tonight."

The words that weren't spoken were *if you come home.* She turned around and walked out of the place without another word.

"Fuck."

He hesitated for a second, glanced back to where Wendy could still be heard cursing and slamming around in the back of her place, then went after Tara. He grabbed the gate and stopped the lift from closing.

As he stepped in, her expression could honestly be called one of shock. He closed the door behind him and pressed the button again for the first floor, only to stop it between floors.

"What are you doing?"

"Giving us a spot to talk. We are always interrupted. So, we'll stay in here." The lift shuddered to a halt and he pinned his gaze on her. "Talk."

"I thought you were discussing something with Wendy."

"You wanted my attention, Tara. I'm giving it to you. All of it, one hundred percent. We're not going anywhere. We're caught between floors. If it takes you all night to tell me, we'll stay here until you do."

"Not really a fan of elevators. Thanks, though."

God, he wanted to hold her. He forced himself to remain on the other side of the space from her because, were he honest with himself, he was thinking about fucking her right here. Not that he didn't care about what she had to say, but because he couldn't look at her and not be turned on. She was perfect to him and he wanted to indulge all his senses in her.

"Talk to me, Tara."

"Can we get out of here?"

"Tara," he said, his patience wearing thin.

"I know I've not been the easiest person in the world to live with." She shrugged. "You know what I mean. Even when I wasn't in your life, I was still there. A pain, doing what I wanted to do without any thought to you or your life."

He wasn't sure what this was leading to and so opted to stay quiet and let her finish. Andrew noticed the tiny sheen of sweat on her brow. He got that she wasn't happy to be trapped in there, but she wasn't making him let her out and he was proud of her for that. But the silence continued too long and he had to break it.

Some strong man I am, can't even outwait her to tell me anything.

"What are you saying?"

"I don't want you to go back to Switzerland."

Hope flared within him.

"I mean…" She rubbed her palms against her hips. "I don't want you to go alone. Or rather *without* me."

Epilogue

Tara crunched on the small carrot stick she'd just plucked from the platter of fresh vegetables and sighed. There was nothing like it in her mind. Outside the large sprawling windows, the sun shone down on the emerald-green grasses that waved in the light breeze.

"I could have done that."

"I don't mind chopping vegetables, Mrs. Hilly. Even my sisters don't think I can mess that up. Well, not too bad, anyway."

The woman gave her a smile, opened the large double fridge and pulled out some pie that she then put out on another counter.

"Just so you know, I love pie too."

"I have another set aside just for you."

"Mrs. Hilly, I think you're deliberately trying to spoil me."

"I pay her extra to do that, you know." Drew poked his head into the kitchen. "Come on, baby. We have to go get your parents."

Joy filled her—she was excited to see them. It had been almost a year. Pushing up on her heels, she kissed Mrs. Hilly before nearly skipping over to Drew's side.

He reached out his hand and she placed hers within it, warmed by something so simple as his touch. Drew pulled her close and dropped a kiss to the tip of her nose. "I love you."

"You are loved."

Once in his car, this time without a driver, she propped her feet up on the dashboard and rolled down the window.

"Thank you for allowing them to come for a visit."

His laugh filled the interior. "Allowed them? Baby, we're family. I love your parents—*our* parents—and welcome any time we get to spend with them."

Angling her head on the seat so she could better stare at him, she smiled. "I'm glad."

He pulled off the road at a park and put them far away from most people there. After stopping the engine, he faced her and took her hand in his.

"How are you doing? I know it's been difficult for you to not have work outside the house."

"I'm good," she replied. "I'm working on passing so I can practice international law and then I will be pounding on the door for the ICC."

"If we have to move closer, then we will. Besides, you'll be Stateside soon and can do some work there if you'd like."

They lived most of the year in Switzerland but lived for a quarter of it at home. She'd not quite been able to cut it out all together. So her parents were coming for two weeks and all four of them were traveling back to the States together.

"I know. You've been nothing but supportive. And while I won't lie and say it's not been hard for me to go from doing what I did as an ADA to being able to sleep in any day I so choose." She undid her belt and inched close enough to kiss him. "Thank you for not giving up on me."

He hooked his finger in the collar of her shirt and tugged before waggling his eyes at her.

"No," she said, shaking her head as if it would add compunction to her statement. "We're on the way to the airport to get my parents. I'm not going there smelling like sex."

"You'd be happy and relaxed." He pulled her closer. "How about I just lick this pussy of yours until you come all over my tongue?"

She whimpered as her clit pulsed and cream gathered in her core. "Drew."

"Just like that," he praised. Before she knew it, his hand was inching up her skirt, giving him access to her freshly shaved pussy. "Fuck, I love you smooth like this. You're so sensitive, especially when you've just been shaved. I love how much you tremble when I lick you. When I push my fingers into you, how you clench around me."

"God, Drew, this isn't fair."

"One taste," he said. "All I want is one taste." His fingertips brushed along her pussy lips and she quivered. "Are you going to deny me? We have time and we'll even get cleaned up before getting them at the airport."

He used his free hand to guide her head toward the back of the SUV. "There's space back there. Or right here."

She shifted and moaned when his fingers touched her with slight brushes between her swollen lips, close but not touching her where she needed it the most. Her clit.

"This isn't fair, Drew." Her voice was breathy. Her entire body gravitated toward him, craving anything and everything he might offer to her.

"Then tell me what you want?" Another of the tantalizing all to brief touches.

"You, inside me." She gave in and undid his pants, reaching in to withdraw his thick length. Then she crawled over him, hitched up her skirt farther and settled over his cock.

"Then put me inside you."

She lowered herself and sighed as he stretched her. Tara knew she'd never get enough of this man. Her love for him grew on a daily basis—yes, they had issues and she didn't doubt more would crop up at some point, but right now, they were together and that was what she needed.

Resting her head against his, she closed her eyes.

"You are loved, Drew."

"As are you, Baroness." He bucked up and she moaned before settling her hands on his shoulders. "Now take what you need."

She took him at his word and did just that.

* * * *

Andrew stared down at the paper in his hand. He wanted to wake his wife and share with her what he'd received today. But she was exhausted. The entire house had fallen asleep after a raucous evening with her parents. Parents who were in the other wing of the house, sound asleep.

Right now, he didn't care if they were or not. Padding back into his bedroom, he smiled as the silvery light from the moon shown down on the woman lying on her side, a pale-yellow sheet pulled up partway over her thigh as she cuddled a pillow against her torso.

Perching on the edge of the bed, he reached out and pushed back a thick chunk of her ebony hair. She stirred but didn't wake.

"I love you so much, Tara. Thank you for loving me enough to stick with me."

God, he wanted to wake her up and share this with her, but he knew better. She had been more tired than usual of late but he knew she'd been studying hard.

"Tara."

"Why are you muttering near me, Drew?"

"You always call me Drew," he commented. "You do know my name is Andrew, right?"

It was a joke between them and she seemed determined to call him Drew.

"I'm fairly certain I know the man I married." She didn't move the pillow, nor did she open her eyes, but there wasn't any doubt she was laughing at him. "Why are you awake at this hour?"

He lowered his head and kissed her shoulder. "I got some news I wanted to share with you."

That opened her eyes. His heart churned over once more at the love in her gaze. "You sound positively giddy. What happened? Wendy quit, or you decide to finally pay her what she's worth and she's staying?"

He popped her on the ass.

"Ohh, so that's what you got. Are we starting something new? Spanking? Knots and ropes?"

His cock jumped in his sweatpants, tenting them out, and he didn't bother to hide any of it.

"I would love to do some of that with you."

She shifted, her body moving sinuously along the sheets. "I'm about to fall back asleep, so tell me then join me."

He stretched out beside her and tapped her on the chin. "I'm going to need you to sit up. You have to read what's on the paper."

With an overly dramatic sigh, she nodded. "Fine." Pushing the pillow at him, she sat while he scrambled to move the item so he could stare at her.

"I think you should be naked at all times."

She shook her head even as her grin grew. "Really? You want me to entertain in my birthday suit?"

"Entertaining me, yes. Yes I do."

Tara waited until he stood up and ran her finger along the length of his cock. "What would be nice is for you to be to drop the sweats and let me suck this cock of yours."

He captured her wrist and drew her away from his dick. Not an easy task, because he wanted to have her hand and lips on him. Stepping back, he retreated for the sheet of paper he wanted her to read. He brought it back to the bed and handed it to her.

She didn't take it, just stared at him.

"Tara."

"Strip and I'll read it. Right now, you have the advantage over me."

"Baby, I don't have any advantage over you, you've always had the advantage over me."

"Drop the sweats, handsome. Then I'll take the paper."

Listening, he did his best to ignore her sharp intake of breath as he removed his pants and stood before her naked.

"Paper."

She cleared her throat. "Right." Beckoning with her hand, she took it from him and scanned it.

Tara furrowed her brow and he wanted to pace, but really, who paced while naked with a hard erection? Many, perhaps, but he wasn't one of them.

She lifted her head. "Is this for real?"

Holding her gaze, he nodded. "Yes."

She launched herself at him and he caught her. Their lips fused as tongues dueled for supremacy. Words faded as he gripped his cock and lined it up to her wetness. Pumping his hips, he pushed deep inside her heat.

Tara sank her hands in his hair and gripped him, holding his face where she wanted it. He took them to the bed, careful not to crush her beneath his larger size. She latched her legs around him, keeping him fully within her body.

Not that he wanted to leave, because he had plans to stay this way for a long, long time. This was his woman — he wasn't going to give her up for anything and would spend the rest of his days making sure she knew how much he loved her.

Capturing control, he wrested it away from her and began thrusting hard and fast into her wetness. Her slick walls held him as she was, tight.

Her mewls became moans and they grew louder still. Baron Andrew Coleman roared with release as his wife screamed his name beneath the moonbeams, her body bowing to his touch. The paper lay on the floor forgotten, the heavy bold print at the top still legible in the soft light.

Welcome Baroness Tara Coleman to the ICC...

**Want to see more from this author?
Here's a taster for you to enjoy!**

Theta Corps: Restitution
Aliyah Burke

Excerpt

The *plip* of water, annoying as it may be, beside his head was the ongoing reminder he still lived. The radiating pain coursing through him was the other aide-mémoire he breathed. It was excruciating to complete the simple task. Calling his situation 'alive' fell into the 'it's a stretch' category.

Ethan Jackson had gone and gotten himself into one hell of a situation.

Rats crawled along his feet and up his legs, biting when and where they chose. He didn't move. There was no point in expending his limited energy in a major attempt to knock the vermin off when they'd just climb back on. Time had long since lost all meaning for him. Other than pain, pretty much everything had. He struggled to remember the faces of his sister and cousin. And his own name.

Heavy footsteps clomped along the damp concrete hall. Every few paces — three — the foot splashed into a puddle. He tensed — either he was losing more time or they were coming back to torture him once more.

Muffled voices reached him as the footsteps stopped. He waited for the door to open, anxious for the tiniest shaft of grimy light to penetrate his world of darkness. After a period of his own warring uncertainty, he noted the footsteps move on. He closed his eyes and attempted to get more rest.

He'd seen the rows of doors each time they'd dragged him to a better-lit room to torture him. He was unsure, however, if there were actual people behind them. Screams — other than his — came occasionally but he'd yet to see another who was being treated in the same vein as him and hadn't given in to the belief there were more prisoners here.

Wherever the fuck I am.

All he recalled with positive clarity was Virginia had been his last definitive location. However, again, that was where the time issue came back into play. He had no knowledge of how long he'd been a prisoner. His struggle to remain alert and strong was more than enough of a challenge. With the rotten food and putrid water, there wasn't much in the way to sustain mental acuity or physical prowess.

The footsteps returned and he forced himself to remain still and not tense.

"Get up!"

He opened his eyes in time to see Hitler's poster boys standing over him and one deliver a powerful kick to his ribs. Movement was slow — no one wanted to hurry to their next bout of torture.

Ethan didn't help much, aware they would drag him up and out of the tiny cell. Sure, his knees got the brunt of it but he conserved energy. True to form, they swore at him in German before yanking him up by his armpits.

All y'all are going to die. I will not die in this cesspool. I'll escape and kill each of you for what you've done to me. His mantra played on a continuous loop in his mind. It offered the slightest bit of hope to his situation.

They dragged him from the cell, his legs sliding over water and other substances he didn't want to think about. He eyed the heavy black boots the two men had, wishing they were on his feet. His own shoes were long gone.

A stone door opened and they entered. Squinting from the light, he gazed around the room. Ethan recognized the man who implemented the torture. His gray linen suit perfectly pressed. Then again, it always was...at the start.

This time there was another in the room. Thin and clad in torn clothing, a black girl stood there holding a tray of something he couldn't see. Not that he wanted to know what it held.

"Mr. Jackson," the man said in a quiet authoritative tone, sliding off his suit coat. "This is going to be our last meeting." He unbuttoned and rolled up his sleeves, the gray vest perfect against his crisp white shirt. "You have been a most amazing volunteer. Your ability to withhold your cries of pain has made you somewhat of a legend."

He pulled on the bottom of his vest. "I wonder if your sister will last as long once she's in my chair. Will her screams be full-bodied or sharp and high? I want to find out. I shudder with anticipation." He grinned. "I will leave you to them. They want to inflict pain on you and we have so few joys out here in the rainforest."

Ethan's blood turned to ice at the mention of his sister. Rage poured into him as if someone had opened the floodgates. He struggled to remain impassive. Internally, however, he killed the German he knew only as Rolf, very meticulous and slow, not to mention with excruciating pain.

He lifted his gaze and focused on the female. She held his gaze, dropping hers to stare at the floor. *I'm in the rainforest.*

"Put him in the chair." The order was barked in German.

Tweedledum and Tweedledee shoved him in the chair then held his arms. He glared at the man who neared, memorizing him so he would be able to find him in the future and kill him. An alarm blared and Rolf pivoted.

"Goddamn locals!" He ran to the door, the two goons following, slammed it shut, locking Ethan in with the woman.

Ethan held himself immobile for a tense moment. Was it a trick? He darted his gaze to her. She continued to stand in the far corner, eyes still on the floor, as if trying to make herself as small as she could or invisible.

He pushed up from the wooden chair, his attention split between her — who appeared a bit older than he'd first believed — and the door. Now that he was upright, he saw some syringes on the tray.

One step toward her then the door crashed open, allowing the Hitler poster boy to barrel into the small cell. Ethan didn't hesitate, just lunged at him and brought him down, digging his ragged nails into the man's eye sockets. While it took him longer than it should have to overpower and kill him, he soon stood, victorious. Blood dripped from his fingers.

He peeked back to the woman on the side. She hadn't moved.

"Come here," he snapped, wiping the blood from his mouth with the back of his hand before he patted down the dead man.

She didn't move.

He ordered her again in German. She lifted her head and sighed softly then shuffled toward him. Her steps were slow, as if she bore some unseen shackles on her thin legs, but her speed—little that it was—remained constant. Ethan took the syringes, checked to make sure they were capped and put them in his pocket. Then he removed the boots and socks of his jailer.

The entire time, alarms blared and she stood like a statue.

"Come," he barked in German.

Again, she listened but he noted her hesitation. He yanked the tray from her hands and tossed it away. Her body jerked and trembled.

What kind of man leaves a woman in with a prisoner? Either she's expendable or the racist fuck trusts her.

He snaked his arm around her neck, grateful his fingers were around the man's assault rifle. He held the side arm in the hand by her throat. "You're my ticket out. Where's the exit? And I will kill you first if you lead me to a trap."

Her body never stopped trembling as she pointed down the darkened passageway. In the back of his mind, he could hear his grandmother's mental reprimand about how wrong it was to treat women in such a fashion. He pressed the muzzle against the junction of her neck and shoulder.

"Don't test me," he commanded in guttural German.

His prisoner never spoke a word as she pointed him to his freedom. Tense, exhausted, he remained alert when they came to a dead end.

He growled under his breath. "I warned you."

She pointed up and he followed with his gaze. A hatch along the wall with a rough ladder built into it.

Ethan pushed his exhaustion to the back of his mind. "We're about to get all kinds of personal. Same rules apply." He shouldered the rifle, pushed her toward the ladder. Shoving the handgun in the front of his nearly destroyed pants, he pressed against her. "You climb with me. Don't be stupid."

Still nothing verbal from her. She reached out and began to climb. He mimicked her, keeping her tight between him and the ladder. At the top, she halted and he reached over her to open the hatch, inch by inch.

Blue sky dotted with white clouds had him squinting as tears sprang to his eyes. After months of near darkness, this sliver of real light bordered on painful. He nudged her up one more step. It wasn't pretty but he got them out.

One hand around her mouth, he closed the door, his gaze darting around. Backing away, toward the thick waiting rainforest, he moved them from the groomed area of the compound.

Voices had him dropping flat to the ground, eyes locked with his hostage, the barrel of the Desert Eagle by her chest between her breasts. No anger was in her eyes, only acceptance of whatever he decided to mete out to her. It rubbed him wrong.

She held his gaze and barely blinked as two men passed by. *Perhaps she's not working with them.* He had a hard time believing these arrogant replicas of the Third Reich would employ—much less trust—a black woman. He moved without delay as the men continued on. *Not very thorough with alarms going off.*

Ethan breathed easier when the rainforest swallowed him up. At least now he had a chance. More alarms blared and he realized his escape had been noted.

A feral grin crossed his face. Time for some payback. He turned to the woman. He ran his gaze over her then around. Stepping away, he took hold of some vines.

"Against the tree."

She didn't argue and he roped her tight with as much speed as he could. Patting his pocket to ensure the syringes were there, he met her gaze. "Keep quiet and I'll come back and cut you free. I have no designs to hurt you if you follow what I say. You help them and I'll kill you as well."

Again, not so much as a sigh. She'd resigned herself to her fate. There went that damn niggling again. He tapped the gun against his cheek as he backed away. He had some men to kill then a home with a life to return to.

* * * *

"Wake up, Mino."

"This better be a damn good reason for you to be in my bedroom, Beauregard."

He kicked her bed frame with one booted foot as he turned on a light. "Come on."

"You breaking into my home is a bit much, don't you think?"

"It wasn't hard. Your security system sucks." Beau stared at the woman glaring at him. Her gaze raked over him before it narrowed.

"You'd better not be bleeding on my floor."

He didn't pause or look to his newest injury. "I need you to take out a bullet."

She tossed back the blankets and slid from her double bed. "They have hospitals, you know. Places where trained people wait to do those kinds of things." She planted her hands on her hips clad in Wonder Woman images and symbols. *Never knew she was into Wonder Woman.*

She yawned. "They even have the proper equipment. Then you wouldn't have sauntered into my dreams."

He lifted an eyebrow.

She held out a hand and waved it at him. "Not what I meant, because I wasn't indicating you were in my dreams. I meant because you interrupted my dreams and—oh, never mind. Let's get this over with so I can go back to sleep."

He trailed her into the small bathroom where he sat on her counter then drew off his shirt.

"You know I'm not a doctor." She removed her eye mask and wasted no time putting her hair up in a ponytail.

"You were in med school." Her gaze snapped to him. "I checked you out. You did three years before—shit!" He jerked his head to where she'd poked his injury. "That hurt."

"My personal life is off limits."

You don't have a personal life. You were sleeping alone on a Friday night. He kept that to himself as she poked and prodded to get out the bullet.

"If you look like this, what do the others look like?"

"Worse."

She grunted. "I won't lie to Masters when he asks."

"I'll be gone by then."

She paused, moving back to peer at him. "You have word on Ethan?"

He stared in her eyes. "Yes."

Mino held his gaze then returned to his injury. "Where is he?"

"Venezuela." Aside from a select few, he'd not shared that with anyone. Mino was one of theirs. Personal secretary to his boss. Someone who had no problem helping them out. But she answered to Masters.

"When do you leave?"

"Soon."

She turned and walked to her bedroom, removing the gloves as she did so. He hopped off and followed, hand over his still-open wound. She was shoving items in a bag.

"What are you doing? I need you to finish this."

She tugged a sweatshirt on then removed the blue cami she'd been wearing, tossing it into a wicker hamper in the corner. "Packing."

"I gathered that," he drawled. "Why?"

After putting on a bra, she shucked her shorts, exchanging them for some hot pink lounge pants. "To go."

"Hell no. You're not coming."

She snorted and grabbed another pack that she checked before nodding sharply. "Let's go. I'll patch you up on the flight."

He took her upper arm as she tried to move by him, one bag over her shoulder and a duffel in the other. "You're not going."

"Yes. I am. Let's go." Defiance sparked in her light-brown eyes.

"I'm not taking care of you in the rainforest."

"Ethan—"

"May not even recognize me."

"He may not but chances are he *will* most likely need medical attention. What were you planning on doing, taking him to the local hospital?" She jerked free of his touch and left the room. She cleaned up her bathroom and waited for him by the door.

Damn. She was right.

Home of Erotic Romance

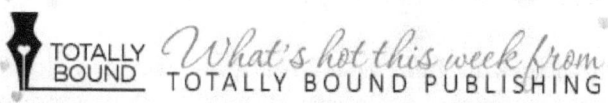

Sign up for our newsletter and find out about all our romance book releases, eBook sales and promotions, sneak peeks and FREE romance eBooks!

https://totallyentwinedgroup.us7.list-manage.com/subscribe/post

About the Author

Aliyah Burke is an avid reader and is never far from pen and paper (or the computer). She is happily married to a career military man. They are owned by six Borzoi. She spends her days at the day job, writing, and working with her dogs.

Aliyah loves to hear from readers. You can find her contact information, website details and author profile page at https://www.totallybound.com